SECRETS IN THE
SHADOWS

LAYNE CALRY

Editing by Angel Blackwood

Cover by Steam Power Studios

ISBN:0692895655
ISBN-13:9780692895658

DEDICATION

To my mom: your unwavering support has kept me going.

To my husband: you listen to me bemoan my characters' fate and my characters and all that entails. I love you.

To Remy: your care, the support you show, and all the time you take to help and walk me through everything. Thank you from the bottom of my heart.

Danielle Cordeau, Danielle Perez, both of you always willing to listen to me rant late at night. You getting me through the highs and lows of writing and everyday life.

Thank you

I love you all.

Acknowledgments

A lot of research went into the writing of this story. The countless hours logged on the computer researching countless fables and myths and legends from all corners of the earth.

I have had many people who have supported me both familial and non. I couldn't have done this without them.

My mother, who has made it her mission to make sure that I am on the right path to success. That I am following the dream I have always wanted. And that I am staying true to myself.

The writer's groups I am a part of. Thank you for broadening my views, showing me where I can improve, and also what I am good at.

And to my editor, who as luck would have it, also became my friend. He is one of the most supportive and patient people I have ever had the pleasure to know, and he makes sure I understand everything.

I owe so many of you.

Thank you for the support.

Prologue

It was with nervous energy that the blonde woman walked back and forth, her eyes on the circle that sat in the middle of the clearing, and standing inside it, her son. She couldn't see him from her vantage point, but she had no doubt in her mind that he would stand there with his large fists clenched and a muscle jumping in his jaw, his brown eyes lowered and lidded in rebellion. As he always did when facing the elders. She rubbed her hands against her linen dress and sighed. She turned to stare into the kind eyes of an older man next to her. He spared a small glance to the young woman next to him, the sole reason for this convergence.

"Does this really need to happen like this? Why can't I help him? I know she has to." The woman jerked her head toward the younger woman. "But why don't I get a bigger role in this? He's my son. I am responsible for him. I did this to him."

The older man smiled softly. "Oh, my dear. You know why. It is fate, destiny, life. Things greater than all of us."

She shook her head and turned back around, a frown on her face. She studied the young woman that stood anxiously behind them, her small frame shivering in the wake of their words. She too held a frown on her beautiful face, and the eyes that she blinked were filled with tears. The mother sighed. *It is so hard to believe that my son, the guardian, that he would need a protector himself, someone to help him. Not to mention that the said protector is a slip of a woman, not quite eighteen. My baby is the keeper and savior of the realm, and he is now reduced to nothing more than a pawn for the council.*

The mother looked away, brushing at her eyes. The back of her throat burned and her body felt overly warm. Tears pushed at the back of her eyes, and a few escaped to fall down her cheeks.

The younger woman stepped forward, worry lines furrowing her brow and tears streaming down her cheeks to mingle in her long hair. Her gaze was intense upon the young man in the circle. The seer turned back to stare at her son, tracing the contours of his face.

"He is so much like his father, both in looks and tortured soul."

This is my fault, this entire mess. Perhaps I should not have borne him, however, even I cannot find an ounce of regret for that action, for the birth of my beautiful son. The seer squeezed her fingers together, digging them into her dress, holding clumps of it in her hands, running it through them. She tilted her head, studying the steepening shadows and her husband's silhouette farther away as he too watched. Her heart fell to her toes as she could see the frown between her husband's eyes. She bit her lip and turned to the waif beside her. The young, innocent thing that wore her heart on her sleeve and the seer's son's in her chest.

The seer spoke sadly, meeting the girl's gaze. "You know, child, there are many ways to save him, but it comes at a deep sacrifice. And it will not be easy. My son bears a stubborn temperament, and it will take you longer to save him than it would another. Are you sure you are willing to bear that burden? That you are willing to sacrifice yourself for his cause? Because he will not let you; it will be a fight for you. You will die just as he does during the final trial if you should fail. And the darkness can and will claim you both."

The long-haired girl turned toward him again and studied him, her face taking on a rosy cast. Then she tightened her tiny jaw and nodded her head.

"I will save him if I can, even at the expense of myself. I love him."

The seer frowned and wiped her eyes swiftly. "This journey, it can take you years or lifetimes.

There will be so much pain and heartache, but I can ease that some."

The seer studied the girl's hardened gaze and touched her cheek with gentle fingers. *I know that she will do this regardless. She will always find him, no matter how stubborn he may be, and he will always be drawn to her, unable to keep her out of his sight. Their souls, their hearts are intertwined in the most ancient of ways, by both true love and fate.*

The girl reached up and squeezed the Seer's fingers and smiled up at her. The Seer nodded her head and with a wave of her hand, she watched as the young lady fell into a sleep from which she would remember nothing. The seer finally allowed the tears to fall as she turned to watch her son.

She spoke to the older man that had stood silent watching the two women's exchange. "He bears the cross of adversity, you know? Mayhap I condemned him when I bore him a halfling, a dark man. The seed of darkness will veil him from view, however, this is a chance he must be given. For he alone is innocent and should not pay for my sins. It isn't fair that fate has given him his own."

The older man shifted and moved forward to touch her shoulder and squeeze a sad smile on his face. "I am so sorry, my dear. And no, you are right. He should not have to pay twice, but we do not make the rules. Fate, ah the three sisters, such interesting women, they have such strange decisions to make." The old man spoke and placed his hand on her shoulder.

"No, we don't make them, but sometimes I wish we did," the seer whispered quietly.

She watched, holding her hand to her cheek, tears falling from her eyes as her son's face contorted with pain and he fell. The smoke burned her nostrils as she watched him fall from her view.

The young man woke up in the alleyway in a haze of pain and no memories. The walls stood near dark and foreboding. He lifted his head, looked around. Large shapes loomed above him. A sign creaked as the wind blew it back and forth. The lights danced in the darkness to add shadows to the already eerie alley. He shivered in the gloom, listening to the lonely water as it dripped down the sides. He watched as things moved through the dimness. An animal snuffled in the trash bins near him, and he grimaced at the sound. He covered his nose as wicked smells assaulted him. A musty odor permeated the air, mixed in with rotten food. He retched, dryly. He reached up to touch his head, while something warm and wet dripped into his eyes. He brushed at the liquid stickiness, trying in vain to stem the flow.

He tried to push himself to his feet but failed. He fell back to the dirt, his cheek landed in mud and wet. He shivered and pushed to get up again, but stumbled. He sighed and closed his eyes until he heard a mewling sound nearby. It touched a chord in his heart. It gave him new energy. Forcing himself to stand, he walked on bruised and weak legs toward the end of the alley, looking for the pitiful sound. Not knowing what drove him to find it but just knowing that whatever it was needed him right now, and he would help it.

Where is it? I can't find it; I need to find it. What is it?

He wrung his hands and stumbled in his hurry and pain, his heart beating a heavy staccato against his prison of skin. Something in the sound called to a vulnerable part of him; he needed to save whatever the creature was that was crying. It sounded weak and alone. He staggered and fell a few times, skinning his knees and his hands but pushing himself to his feet again, crying out in agony each time.

He finally found the source of the noise: a small kitten, a tom cat that was missing the tips of his ears and the skin around his face was puckered and raw as if he had been skinned alive, but the nose and its eyes stayed untouched. The young man picked it up and snuggled it. The animal's blood mixed in with his, but he didn't care.

He lurched toward the bright lights and voices at the end of the alley, and he held tightly to the cat, oblivious to the cerise that ran down his arms and hands. He blinked blood from his eyes.

He stood swaying underneath the light,

watching the blue and red lights of the police cars and their occupants. An officer saw him and ran over to him with a gasp and grasped his forearms, holding him up and steady. The officer motioned for another to come over, and they gently took the kitten from the boy's hands, wrapping it warmly in a small blanket. The dark young man winced and tried to pull from the officer's embrace, reach for the cat.

"What's your name, boy? What happened to you?" the police officer pestered him with questions. The young man shook his head with a groan. His ears rang.

He stared at the officer's face, trying to answer him, but his tongue felt stuck to the roof of his mouth and his chest tight. He winced and again tried to pull away, but he couldn't. His body felt weak and raw.

He looked down and away from the bright lights, thoughts and memories assailing him, all moving like a slow-motion movie across his eyelids. His mother, blonde hair and blue eyes, a man, a man with a knife, then blood, and his name. Ryder, perhaps it was, and then darkness, sharp pains assailed him throughout his body, his back, his arms, and then a knife whispered through the air, coming to rest on his cheekbone.

He finally pulled his arm from the officer's grasp. Ryder reached up to trace the slash across his face and then the thought was gone as quickly as it had come. He stared at the red streaks across his fingers and then moved his gaze upwards. He looked at the police officer questioningly and with furrowed brow.

"I don't know, sir, but it's my birthday." Then with a swift wobble, he reeled and the ground rushed to meet him as his world went black.

Chapter 1

Ryder

Ryder Greer stood like a dark shadow surveying the area around him. He studied it as one would look at land to buy. If one did not look twice, he almost wouldn't be noticed. The darkness of his clothes blended in perfectly with the walls on either side of him. The glaring sun, however, lit up the front of his face, showing that a person stood there. He didn't move at first, his arms hanging motionless at his sides. He shook his head and looked down, a frown etched on his face. He couldn't make himself step into the sunlight and toward the new job waiting for him.

I just need a moment to gather myself. To calm down. I am home again. So many questions. And so different yet the same. Nothing looks familiar.

Ryder lifted his gaze to read the expressions on

everyone's faces. Drinking in their hopeful expressions. His heart twisted painfully at the broken-down ones. He knew that look well. He snorted as they scurried hither and yon, on their way to or from class he wasn't sure. Like a hive of busy bees.

As they walked, their shadows would block the sun from his face. However, every little bit, the light would flash across his jaw, lighting up a scar that wore a path from his right temple to his lower jaw. He blinked at the heat on his face, the flare of hot on the scar, the momentary pain that came with it, and turned away from the sun. He traced his fingers down the scar, cooling it with his touch. The one remainder of a life-changing day, nine years ago, when he lost everything. He didn't even realize the cut that had gone to the bone was there most days; he wore it well. It was a part of him now.

A bone-weary sigh rattled from his chest, and as the final school bell tolled, he rolled his shoulders and stepped forward. With a deft flick of his wrist, he swung the frayed backpack onto his shoulder. Ryder gave one last cursory glance around, and then he joined the throng of college students.

Ryder winced at the sound of his new boots on the pavement. He stared at the offending shoes, thinking longingly of his old worn in pair. These ones were too stiff, too hard. His others were soft and supple, perfectly broken in, contouring to his feet. However, though comfortable, they were not a good fit for his first day on a new job.

He pulled himself up short when a small waif of a woman stopped dead in her tracks. He backpedaled quickly so as not to crush her by running into her. She stood still, staring at the campus grounds and buildings. Ryder frowned, about ready to ask her to move when her tightly coiled body caught his attention. He bit his tongue instead and studied her. She held herself immobile, her arms firm against her sides. He knew that look well, a woman about to panic. He had worn that face, felt that tightening. He brushed hands at his chest, remembering the feeling well.

He watched her, his mouth slightly parted in surprise as she slowly took a deep breath and calmed herself and when she turned, his heart lurched to his throat as she smiled. It was a smile of complete and utter joy, like a punch to the gut; it stole his breath. It caught deep in his chest, and he gasped. It was an elation the likes of which he had never seen, if his few memories were anything to go by, that was.

His nostrils flared at the innocence that wafted from her; it was pure and unadulterated. He tilted his head, studying the lines on her face and the gentle weariness that lay on her shoulders. For one so happy, she was very careworn. The gentleness of her countenance touched a tender, defenseless spot in his chest. He grunted softly, shaking his head forcefully and turned away as swiftly as was possible, biting his tongue to keep from speaking.

To ask if she was okay.

Ryder was about to walk away when someone called out a name, Xeraphina. He turned and studied the waif he had almost run into. In a moment of déjà vu, he wondered at her name and why he felt like he knew it. He traced the risen ridges of his scar, trying to form his muddled thoughts together. It was a small echo of something, a tendril of a memory or a thought, and it threatened to overtake him. So many of them lately, but he could not grasp them nor hold onto them. Like smoke, they always wafted away.

Always disappearing, these thoughts I have, and what I can only guess at memories.

Ryder shook his head and instead turned to gaze at the man that had uttered the young woman's name. Ryder snorted and had to quickly quell the sound, averting his gaze from both. The other man's light blond hair and hazel eyes made Ryder think of an oversized cherub child.

I bet he is considered handsome to most of the women and possibly even some of the men on this campus. I think he looks ridiculous and fake. There is no personality to him, no real depth. Just good looks and a smirk on his face. His brain is probably as dull as that stupid look on his face.

"Hello, Duff," the young woman murmured to the blond man, and she smiled again. Ryder took a shuddering breath, calming his jumpy insides and cooling his warm head. As she turned away, Ryder took another deep breath and swept his hand over his burdened face. There was no reason for such a reaction to a woman he had never met before, nor had he ever spoke to her.

Ryder stood still and stalwart after the two walked away. He rubbed his eyes, digging at the bridge of his nose, forcing the strange sense of loss and foreboding that had risen to grip him. The young man growled, trying to force the strange thoughts away. The other man's name, Duff, it tickled at his conscience, digging into the back of his mind, but he had no idea why. Ryder returned his gaze to the two students, assuming they were lovers. Try and find a reason for the tense feelings deep within him, but he could remember nothing. Ryder shook his head and, squeezing his fingers into the shoulder straps of his backpack, he stepped further away. He was certain now that it was nothing more than the nervousness of embarking on a new journey, where his life had begun.

Ryder glanced at his watch and scowled. *Great, I'm late. I hate being late for work, especially on the first day of the new job. Frigging beautiful.*

The campus library came into view. Ryder smiled and stopped. He dug his fingers into the straps of his pack. The tall doors were gilded in wood and gold. The tiny bell tower that sat atop let the campus know when classes would change. It was beautiful, and Ryder had to take a minute to still the beating of his heart as he gazed upon it. Ryder traced the contours of the words laced in black against the wooden grain with soft fingers.

Byhall University Library. He walked through the large doors, his hands sliding along the cool metal of the handles. There were books everywhere, and his heart tightened at the sight. Ryder stopped where he was and stared in awe, inhaling deeply the smell of old pages and leather bound words. There was nothing the giant of a man coveted more than knowledge itself and reading. And here in this library, he had the freedom to read them all if he so desired as long as his work was done. Ryder gave one last sniff and, trailing his fingers down their spines, he trudged toward his new boss's office.

As Ryder walked, he wondered if the books within these walls would help him, if they would give him the answers he had been seeking.

Will I find more information here about the infliction that plagues me? The reason for my lost memories of my mother and my childhood? I hope so. I'm tired of blankness. I was seventeen. I should be able to remember more than I do. I don't know why the memories won't commute; not even doctors could tell me. I will figure it out. I will find out what happened all those years ago.

Ryder stepped anxiously forward, his thoughts focusing back on his boss and the late time. His palms sweaty, he rounded the corner. He really needed this job and the connections it held. This was a doorway to finding out his life before.

Ryder rounded the corner and came to the tall oak door with the Mr. G. Hennessey in gilded letters on the front. He raised a large, calloused hand to knock, but the door pushed open, almost catching him on the chin before he could stop it. Ryder moved back, his nostrils flaring. He stared at his new boss, taking in the older man's appearance.

A small smile upturned the corner of his mouth. No matter how many times he saw the Professor, his appearance made him chuckle. He reminded Ryder of a grasshopper. Mr. Hennessey was smaller than Ryder by a good bit, with brown, bespectacled eyes. His manner was curious as was his gaze, peering from a squashed and wizened face, and he wore a woolen brown suit.

Ryder tilted his head, unsure why the man would wear such a suit in August, but Ryder held out his hand anyway to shake the man's, a smile pasted on his face. Mr. Hennessey grasped his hand in his firm grip.

"Ryder, my boy. Always good to see you. Glad to have you on."

Ryder cringed and fought the urge to clap hands over his ears as the man's boisterous voice rebounded on the walls. Ryder frowned but squeezed the man's hand in return. Ryder was unaccustomed to such a bold sound, and he briefly wondered how a curator of a library was so loud.

He must be making up for his height. It's the only thing that makes sense. Compensation.

Ryder curbed his tongue, wanting to ask about the tone of his voice, instead, he spoke quietly. "Hello, sir. I apologize for my lateness. I was enjoying the morning air."

Ryder shifted at the slight lie, a trickle of unease skittering up his spine.

It's my own fault, but I can't tell my new boss a girl's smile knocked me breathless or that she and her boyfriend's names tickled my conscious and I'm so hungry for answers I stopped to stare and wonder.

Ryder took a step back, smiling as Mr. Hennessey spoke, using his hands to emphasize his words.

"Nonsense, young man. Morning air is a wonder, a pleasure. It's the small things. We won't be busy today anyway. First day of term and all that."

Mr. Hennessey shook his head and grabbed Ryder's arm and tugged it gently as he walked past.

"Come, come, Ryder. A tour is in order, show you our small reading and book haven."

Mr. Hennessey looked back, a smile his face, it lit up his eyes. "Not much here as you are probably used too, I'm afraid. What with your extensive background, knowledge, and degrees? You've traveled the world. I heard you spoke with guardians of some of the lost civilizations. A historian, professor, genealogist, and librarian, we are blessed. It warms my heart to have you here. We will make good use of you, mark my words. An asset to our humble library."

The man bounced down the hall. Ryder snorted as he found himself nearly doing the same thing. He caught himself, and instead slid fingers deeper into his pockets and followed behind the librarian.

"Your usual run of the mill library," Mr. Hennessey called back to Ryder, trailing his fingers along the spines of the books. A move that delighted Ryder, who felt a kindred spirit with the man. The man pointed to an oak desk in the foyer.

"Here's your new desk area. They tell me many an author sat there. I don't imagine you will have much time to enjoy it, though. Which is unfortunate. I imagine you have a tale or two. Especially once we really get busy in here."

Ryder shook his head. "I have not lived a life nearly as exciting as you make it sound, sir."

The old man smiled and patted the tabletop, He tilted a pencil holder to the left and aligned it with the other items on.

Ryder shoved his hands deep into his pockets as he watched and felt the ever burn of an itch to touch everything. There was nothing more delightful to the man than the firm feeling of a book in his hand and the smell of the pages. There was something about the scent of them, it put the images into his head and smelled divine. He shook his head.

I need to pay attention. Cannot let my mind wander onto the things that I could read.

"This here's the religious studies area." The old man patted a nearby column.

"A lot of my own students will need this section for my class. Please do remember that. Now, rule-breakers aren't tolerated here, Knowledge is power so we must be careful who comes and who learns and who listens."

Ryder blinked and stared at him. He frowned. "Doesn't everyone deserve a chance at learning?"

Mr. Hennessey dipped his head and rubbed his chin. "Well yes you could argue that point and it is true. However, some people use knowledge to their advantage you know. I wouldn't want anyone that disrespects this library or you in here."

Mr. Hennessey cleared his throat and looked at his watch. "Oh, dear me. I must be going. Make yourself comfortable young Ryder."

Ryder watched the man leave, confused at the last exchange.

Now, what would he have meant by that?

Everyone deserves to know the world. And everyone can be taught respect. I would rather someone was here learning than out there. If he could see some of the children throughout the world. Who cannot learn, who do not have that luxury. I was almost one of them.

Ryder shifted and turned as he felt the hair on the back of his neck stand up. He stared at the tall gabled windows, the tables, and the cases. He sniffed and turned his head as quick as he could. He could smell smoke. What was on fire. He stared at the wall certain that something lurked behind it. A young man came around from the stacks and stared at him.

Ryder studied him, taking in the clothes and the backpack the deer in the headlights look.

"I'm sorry sir. I need to check this book out."

Ryder took another sniff and all he smelled was paper and wood. He gave a shaky smile. "Of course. And no smoking in the library."

The kid stared at him, his mouth dropped open. He grabbed his book, rapidly walked out the door.

I need to watch some of these students more carefully it would seem. I wonder why he didn't smell of smoke?

Ryder walked to the shelf ad looked around, for the telltale sign of smoking, ash or lingering smoke. He saw nothing. He scratched his head and shrugged.

Must have filtered inside then. I will have to tell that boy sorry for accusing him. Though he should have spoken up.

Chapter 2

Xera

Xera slid into her seat, brushing a strand of long brown hair from her cheek. She placed her bookbag on the floor and pulled a notebook and pencil from inside. Settling them just so and nicely lined up together on her desk, she studied the classroom and those around her with a hint of a smile on her face. So many interesting people to look at and study.

She shifted, looked around for the teacher anxious and excited to get the religious studies class started. A topic near and dear to her heart. She had always been curious about other religions, her own faith being so strong within her. Xera started in surprise when her neighbor sat down near her, a smirk always present on his baby face.

"Duff? I had no clue you were taking this course. I thought you hated all things religious."

Duff leaned back in his chair, lacing his fingers behind his head. "Oh, you know, Xera, the view is all that matters. And besides, I have to take this course and pass it if I want to graduate someday. I honestly don't know how this has anything to do with my degree, but eh."

He grinned at her and winked at another nearby student and was rewarded with a soft titter of amusement. Xera snorted and turned back around. He had always been the everlasting playboy. What did she expect, though, given the family he came from and the strange life he led?

Xera frowned and looked at her watch and then the door, wondering where her professor was. It had been some time since she had been to school and never college, but she had thought that a professor would be at least punctual of all things. Xera turned to ask Duff as he had been at the campus for a semester longer and found him arms deep in conversation with the girl next to them. She shook her head and sighed, turning back around, she smiled with relief when the small professor came into view.

Xera covered her mouth, holding in a giggle at his apparel and looks. He was clearly very short in stature and had large brown eyes behind huge glasses. He reminded her a bit of a bug with a squashed face, and though it made her want to giggle, she couldn't help but notice that his countenance seemed kind and wise. She marveled at the rich energy that was held just beneath his surface, clear in the way he bounced on the balls of his feet, excited to get the day started.

The professor cleared his throat and stood straight as the class got quiet and sat to attention. "Good morning to you all. I am Dr. Hennessey, and I am your professor. I plan to expose the knowledge you hold hidden in your brains and broaden on it in this class. And I will tell you right now, I dearly love written reports, you never really know what you may find out about yourself while writing and reading. That being said, you will become closely acquainted with our current librarian, Ryder."

Xera had to cover a small snort of laughter as a collective groan went throughout the classroom when written reports were mentioned. The name that followed, however, had her freeze in midair. She tugged at a strand of her hair.

Ryder? I know that name? Such an unusual name, not one you here very often. Hmm a bit like mine I suppose, but Ryder.

She was tugged from her thoughts by the professor. She shook her head and smiled, putting the silliness behind her.

Probably just heard the name before.

Dr. Hennessey held up his hands and spoke over the noises. "Now, now there will be none of that. Writing is fun, you'll see. Now, let's begin with roll call, shall we?"

Xera listened to the many names in front of her as she doodled in the edges of her syllabus. She was surprised out of her reverie with a soft noise from the professor.

"Hmm, oh my, that is a name I haven't seen in quite some time."

The professor looked up, his eyes twinkling as they settled on Xera. "Miss Xeraphina McCall."

Xera returned his smile, though slightly baffled by the exchange, and she raised her hand. The professor smiled and gave her a small bob of his head. "Please, call me Xera."

Mr. Hennessey chuckled and spoke. "Oh delightful, delightful. Xera it is." He bent to the task of writing her nickname beside her name, or so Xera assumed.

Xera sat back in her seat as the professor continued to call out names. Xera watched his face. She smiled at the full expressions that danced across it. He was a man that wore his emotions on his face for all to see. Something that fascinated Xera as she was the same way. She was surprised when his jovial smile was replaced with a frown, and he looked up his gaze sweeping across the many faces, and he settled on one. Xera turned her gaze to Duff and then back to the professor, startled that the frown was for Duff.

"Duff Mickaffee." Xera looked over at him and was appalled at the smirk on his face. To treat a professor with such disdain, it was not suiting. She sighed, though, and shook her head. She shouldn't have expected anything less. He raised his hand. Xera watched as the professor and he stared at each for a long beat of a moment and then they both broke eye contact.

He had to have taken this course before and didn't do well. That is the only reason for such a reaction from a professor and himself. His mother should have taught him more manners instead of letting him run rampant through town and roughshod over everyone.

Xera shook her head. It wasn't her place to wonder about the professor and Duff's history. And besides, it was most likely a repeat class for Duff and he hadn't gotten along with the professor. Duff wasn't the easiest to get along with, and if his mother got involved, anyone who messed with her precious baby, well, she could only imagine the irritation there.

As professor Hennessey continued the roll call, Xera took her wandering gaze to the syllabus in hand. Her first paper was due in October, perhaps she should consider the library.

A guilty pleasure anyway, so pass the class and do something I enjoy. Win win. Besides, a male librarian, not that they are an uncommon occurrence, but it is certainly not usual around here. All my librarians were old little biddies with glasses and scowls.

Xera walked from the cold school halls into the hot August sun. She shuddered at the chill that lit her body at the sudden change in temperature. Duff was at her heels. She was startled from her thoughts by his words.

"My God, could that class be any more annoying? And that professor, did you see him? Those glasses and he bounces around like a little school boy."

Xera turned to look at him, a frown between her brows.

"It's only the first day, Duff. Anything could happen. And you shouldn't be so rude; he is your professor after all. I liked his exuberance."

Duff scoffed.

"You would. Yeah right. Religions and organizations give me the heebies. Naw, I'll be glad when the semester is over. Second times the charm, anyway right? And so, who cares if he is my teacher? Doesn't mean anything. He still looks goofy. He's going to break a hip he isn't careful."

He patted Xera on the back. "Ah right, I'm off."

Xera watched him go, wondering how they were even friends. She shuddered in the heat, feeling eyes on her. She curled her hands around her arms. She looked back once and hurried to her next class.

Xera pushed the large doors on her building and tightened her grip on her backpack. She had one free period before her next class. She drifted along the campus with not much thought to her destination. She found herself standing in front of a large building. A glance up and she smiled: the library. She took large steps to the door and stood still, tracing fingers along the letters on the front door. Books were wonderful, her kryptonite. Her breathing hitched and goose bumps curled around her arms. She shivered in anticipation. Xera pushed open the doors of the charming library, the familiar smell of paper wafting toward her. A soft smile hovered around her mouth. She broke the silence with a squeak of surprise when she came face to face with a dark giant of a man.

She had seen him earlier but not this close and not in front of her; he had been behind. He sat in the chair, long limbs over top of the desk. She covered her mouth to stifle a gasp at his height. The sheer space he took up was intimidating. However, he was beautiful, and she forgot herself for a moment. She curled her arms behind her back, trying to search for the right thing to say or do. She studied the way his long legs were propped and the curious gaze that met her own over top of the paperback in his hand. Her breath caught in her throat at the gems of melted coffee with animalistic fervor peeking out.

The moment was marred as the door was pushed open from behind and the librarian sucked in a sharp breath of irritation. Xera turned to see Duff stepping in with a smirk on his face. She supposed he would have that effect on people if they didn't know him. He seemed to ooze trouble, and it always found him. He wasn't the easiest to get along with.

"Hello, Duff. What brings you to the library? You hate to read."

Duff gave her an ornery grin. "Just looking for the prettiest girl on campus."

Xera chuckled but shook her head, knowing he wasn't serious in any way. She turned back to the librarian to find him standing. He towered above them both, and he had a raised brow.

"Can I help the two of you?"

Xera shifted at the quiet yet authoritative words the librarian spoke. She shifted the tension in the air between the two, thick. She stared at Ryder for a moment, her mouth slightly parted. The dark promises his lilt offered made her shudder. Something was strange about this librarian, something primitive, and she was uncertain how to take it.

Xera shook her head, ashamed at her thoughts. How dare she think such things about a man she had never met. To call him a wild man, it was rather rude of her, and she wasn't quite sure how to go about changing her way of thinking.

He moved closer to them and a small squeak worked its way from her mouth again at his sheer presence. He had a commanding air to him. Horror quickly replaced her awe as he looked at her first with confusion and then anger. It was only then that she caught sight of the scar that marred his face. She felt the telltale burn of shame slide across her cheeks and into her hairline.

Ugh, how terrible. He must think I was making a noise because of his scar. It is a rather large and ugly one, but he carries it well. Poor thing. How awful of me. It really wasn't his scar, he's just so large. He's even bigger than Duff, and I thought Duff was large. And look at that hair, as black as a raven's wing and just long enough. I bet he runs his fingers through it all the time.

Xera wrinkled her nose, detecting a slightly hidden accent under his timbre. Trying to recall where it was from. She tilted her head. It sounded like the old English heard in movies of begotten times. It suited him. She nodded her head. Yes, it definitely suited him. Xera touched hands to her cheeks as a heated stain covered them, and she bowed her head, appalled at her own behavior and thoughts.

How can I go from feeling so terrible to wondering about his voice? I think I need to get some sleep or something. I am being foolish.

She lifted her gaze and met his bemused one and shook her head. "Forgive me. I was lost in my own thoughts. I'm Xera, and this is Duff. I was just looking for something to do in my free time, and I love the library, so here I am."

She finished the last part lamely and waited for the man to say something, anything to save her from embarrassment.

Xera reached up to tug on her ears as the heat flared higher when the librarian smiled at her. It was a smile that stole her breath and lit up Ryder's entire face and his eyes twinkled at her. She was, however, lost in the next moment when his smile was replaced with a frown and a scowl deepened the lines between his eyes. Xera frowned, she searched his face,

What could make someone be happy one minute and miserable the next? He seems wounded, like a wild animal. But there's something about him. I know him, or at least I feel like I do.

Xera was thrown from her thoughts as the librarian turned around and motioned for them both to follow him. "I am Ryder. Come this way. The fiction section is this way. If you want to kill some time, that would be the place I would go. There are some amazing stories hidden in there. Faraway places and dreams come true. Much better than the reality of homework and studying, and well, reality. My favorites are the stories about were-animals."

Xeraphina got lost in his honey, melt in your mouth voice and realized with yet another blush to her cheeks that he had stopped and was pointing to a bookshelf. Smiling to herself and moving out around him, she began to peruse the books, anything to keep both the librarian and Duff from seeing her crimson cheeks.

Xera turned with a book in her arms to find the librarian had departed, and she stared into the darkened face of Duff. She looked at him and then away, to turn back and the look was gone. Xera gulped. She wasn't sure what was going on, but it must have just been a trick of the light. Duff wasn't normally an angry fellow of any sort. If anything, he was irritatingly happy all the time. She nodded to herself. Yes, it had to have just been a trick of the light.

She held out the book to show him the title: Jane Eyre. "This is one of my favorites. Do you want to pick out one?"

Duff gave her a strange smile, off-kilter. He

shook his head, his wheat blonde hair moving across his forehead in an arc. "Naw, I'm not much of a reader. I just came in with you. I told you I'd keep an eye on you, promised your mom too before she passed. Remember?"

He teased her, but she nodded her head yes. She remembered.

"I doubt much could happen to me in a library, but thank you."

Duff shrugged. "You never know, that librarian looks a little shifty."

Xera chuckled and shook her head. "Oh, he does not. If you aren't getting a book, let's go. I want to get this one home and start reading it again. I should really buy a copy."

Folding the book back into her arms, she made the short trek back to the librarian's desk. She arrived before he noticed her, and she took the moment to study him more closely. There was a small lock of hair that kept sliding to the middle of his forehead. It made him look like a strangely-sized little boy. She smiled to herself and jumped when he spoke.

"Can I help you with anything else? Any questions?"

She shook her head and held the book out to him. He smiled at her, a teasing half-smile, and studied the cover of the book, handling it as if it were a priceless treasure.

"Ah, Jane Eyre. One of Bronte's better ones, I think." He ran it through the scanner and held it out to her with a smile. "Due back in three weeks, Miss McCall."

Xera held the book with shaky hands and, dipping her head, she left the library and the librarian that made her think too much and blush even more.

Way to go, Xera. He must think you are insane or at the very least a silly young girl. What is wrong with me?

Xera froze when she realized she was rushing away from Duff as well as the library. She turned around. She met Duff's eyes and reached out, but she stopped before she met his arm.

She frowned. "I'm sorry, Duff. I guess today just has me all fuddled." Duff stood silent behind her, and he gave her half a smile. Which made her feel even worse.

"No worries, Xera. I have to get to class anyway. And the first day of college can do that to you if you aren't careful. I hope you get the hang of it, soon. See ya."

Duff gave her a small wave and headed the way they had just come. Xera frowned. She didn't think there was a building that way. She shrugged and turned away, the skin on the back of her neck crawling in unease again. She looked around, certain she was being watched, but finding no one, she shivered and increased her speed, anxious to get away from the uninviting area.

CHAPTER 3

TAMESIS

A young woman sat in the shadows watching as Xera spoke with first Ryder and then Duff. The end of the cigarette she held between two ruby lips was the only thing visual. It flared a brilliant orange as she inhaled and then blew the smoke outward to watch it linger and then disappear.

The other woman smiled devilishly to herself. That Ryder, he was a most handsome creature, so charming and oh so fine.

Oh, the things I could do to that man, it would curl that jet black hair of his. He wouldn't know what hit him.

Tamesis gave a grim smile. Giggling high and girly, she took a minute to stretch and wink at the man next to her as he openly stared at her. The man turned away and an ugly look passed across Tamesis's face. A noise of disgust rose high in her throat as she watched Xera, the perfect little tart, walk away as rapid as her gimpy leg could take her. Tamesis snarled to herself.

"Those two, they know nothing of their destiny and their fate, oh but they will. Just you wait, both that perfect little tart and her law-abiding picturesque soldier. They don't know the things that I could do to them, to him. Oh, the things I could do to him."

She scoffed again under her breath. She could do things, but she couldn't grab a hold of him, and there was no desire to. Her heart was already laid claim. And none could break that chain. It went against all the ancient laws.

Tamesis clicked her long red nails against the tabletop, scratching a T in the marble table. "Oh, I'll have my day. Just you wait you stupid little bitch. You may have had such a movie-like life, but I'll make sure you rue that day when the time comes. It was no bed full of roses, but it was much better than mine."

Tamesis frowned and shook her head, anger burning like acid in the back of her throat. It just wasn't fair. Xeraphina McCall had the life dreams were made of, at least mostly, and her beauty lay unmarred, but not Tamesis's. Tamesis traced the scars that took up her cheeks.

"Oh she'll give me what I want in the end, both of them will, and they won't even realize they are. I will make sure of it."

Tamesis stood, a high-pitched, cold giggle in her throat as she ground out her cigarette on the nearby tabletop. Throwing a few dollars down and swallowing her drink, she turned away with a twitch of her skirt. Chuckling darkly, she held her head higher at the nearby looks she drew from the people of masculine persuasion.

Oh, how I love the power of long legs and a short skirt. Look at the way they part like the red sea. I can have whatever I want. It's just too bad so many others don't know their true potential. I could have shown Xera the truth. Could have given her lessons. We could have been friends, but no. No, she doesn't deserve it. I deserve it all. Oh, I'll make a name for myself yet. Me, Tamesis Jade, it will be amazing.

Chapter 4

Ryder

Ryder stood staring out into the steepening shadows. He sighed. His first day was done. He reached behind him and rubbed at the knot that stood hard and cruel at the back of his neck. Hours of bending over books and the computer were not good for his six foot eight frame and the muscles that held it up. Ryder moved and grimaced as he shifted the rubbing from his neck to his chest. He dug at the burning and tightening there, anxious about it, but guessing it was nothing more than indigestion. He shouldn't have had that burrito. He sighed and dug deeper, the pain growing tighter. Ever since he ate lunch and then saw that little college girl – Xera was her name – and her boyfriend. What a sight they were. He snorted and shook his head.

There is something about her, though. I feel like I know her, that I am supposed to meet her. Which is ridiculous honestly, but I know her.

A small laugh shook his frame, and he paused in his ministrations to look down and catch sight of the furry felines that hung there about his feet. He blinked and smiled down at the tabby tomcat and his long-haired white female friend.

Bending down toward them, he brushed fingertips along their backs, marveling at their soft purring and arching into his hand. He paused to curl his palm around the tabby and lift him to his face. He rubbed the tabby and ran his foot along the female. Burying his face into the tabby's fur, he spoke to them both, an undercurrent of laughter in his voice.

"Hello, Aspasia. My toes are not your toy mouse, stop that. And Aristotle, how good you look today, friend."

Ryder lifted his face from Aristotle's back and ran his thumb and forefinger along the raised scars that made up the creature's face. He rubbed them until he purred with exultant joy.

"I have had an interesting day today, Aris. There is so much happening, perhaps it was a mistake to come here in search of answers. Maybe I wasn't ready for them. Because I'll tell you, this morning I was on my way to work. I wish you could come too, Aristotle."

He chuckled as his friend pushed against his chin in search of more cuddles.

"Oh stop it you silly cat. Listen to me."

Aris tilted his head, letting loose a soft meow. Ryder continued. "Anyway, I was on my way to work and this girl and her boyfriend were there, and I had to stop because she was so happy, Aris. I have never seen anyone so happy before. And she looked so familiar and her name, Xeraphina, I know I've heard it before, I know it. But I cannot for the life of me place it."

Ryder shifted and shook his head, moving his furry pal from his hand to the crook of his arm as he walked toward the kitchen. He continued to pat his head while he lay his musings out loud.

"I was late to work. Can you believe it? Me. All because this woman looked so familiar. But it is more than that. And I don't have the words for it, Aris."

Ryder laughed. "Don't look at me like that, cat. Yes, I know. Yes, there was something about her that made me want to save her."

Ryder looked at the cat in his arms as the creature stared up at him, his large, green eyes wide in his head. Ryder smiled shakily and shook his head, pushing the offending feeling of vulnerability down. He never understood why he always had this knack for knowing when someone was in trouble, or at least had come from trouble. But he did, and he always wanted to save them.

He sighed and touched his pal's nose. "I know I can't save all the strays, Aristotle. I know that, and I know I shouldn't try, but I just can't help it. Perhaps it is because I wish someone had saved me?"

Ryder sighed and placed the cat on the floor as he reached for his coffee cup. He turned and walked back to the living room, Aristotle and Aspasia weaving through his feet. He settled into the nearby armchair and gave a small smile at the tabby when he jumped to the arm of the chair.

"There was something off about that boyfriend of hers, Aristotle. I am telling you, darkness bled from his pores if you know what I mean. I disliked him on sight. There is just something evil about him."

Ryder snorted. "Don't look at me like that, cat. I know I read too much, but it's the truth. He's not right. Just the sight of him made me so angry. It made me want to break things, and you know very well, that I do not like to lose my temper."

The cat gave a soft growl and attacked Ryder's finger as he was pointing it. He shook his head and pulled his hand back. "Hey, how rude." Ryder laughed as the cat batted at him again, and he held up a hand. "Okay, I'll be quiet now. How about some TV?"

Ryder turned to the television and sat still, putting on an old favorite movie, but his mind wandered back to the girl and the day he had.

I liked how she said my name. It was comfortable on her tongue as if she has said it before. I liked the familiarity. I don't get that often. Too much moving, though I suppose that is my own fault, never wanting to stay anywhere for too long. I do like it that way, but one does get lonely sometimes. I don't know why I am so affected; this is ridiculous. After all, she proved she was the same as the others, gasping at my scar. I forget it sometimes, and God, if there is even one, feels fit to remind me that I am not normal.

Ryder scoffed at the bitterness that rose inside of him and shook his head. Aristotle let loose a loud cry at being shoved from the armrest when Ryder had grasped it, and he flounced away. Ryder frowned and reached toward Aristotle. His cheeks burned at his reaction.

"I'm sorry, Aristotle. Apparently, the residual feelings are still there. If you could have seen her face, though, when she caught sight of my scar. Those bright blue eyes of hers got wide, and her smile faltered. It was disheartening, let me tell you. And she was such a tiny thing, so fragile, and she looked up at me like I was going to break her. And I would never. I don't like being viewed as a monster."

Ryder tightened his hand into a fist and shook his head. "I bet it's that boyfriend of hers, that pretty boy on the outside, monstrous on the inside.

You remember the one. You and me, we always remember those kind, don't we? I would never hurt her or any woman for that matter. To be looked at like I would." Ryder shook his head and searched the dim light for his cat.

Aristotle stood in the corner staring at him from the shadows, his tail twitching. "Oh, come on, don't be that way."

Ryder held out his hand, and a slow smile worked its way across his mouth as the cat feigned disinterest but moved closer to him and then hopped back to the chair.

"You always listen, Aristotle. I think the time is long overdue for a shower. Let's find the other girls, Aris."

Ryder stood and placed his cup in the sink. He meandered throughout his small cottage looking for the other two cats he shared his abode with, but he was brought up short by the image he saw in the mirror when he walked past it to the shower.

"No wonder she was scared of me. Look at that, Aris. I am covered in all sorts of scars. I supposed they would frighten most people. I am just used to them by now."

Ryder stared at the raised, ropy scars that took up most of his back, two lines the whole way down, raw and pink. As if he had been whipped with a burning hot whip in two straight lines over and over again. He curled his lip and shook his head.

Such ugly things.

Sweat beaded along the top of his upper lip as he traced them with gentle fingertips. Marveling that they didn't hurt.

"It's a wonder I am still alive, isn't it? Perhaps it's a good thing I can't remember much of anything before I was 17. Because whatever happened to me was horrific. The scars are testament to that."

Ryder frowned and tightened his hand, feeling the ever-telling burn at the back of his head that meant he was getting angry. Angry at his past, angry that he knew nothing, angry at the world. He took deep, even breaths, trying to dispel such darkness from his mind and heart. He settled to the toilet, his head on his hands propped to his knees.

This is awful. I came for answers, but what if I get them? What then? There will be anger I imagine, because honestly, how could anyone let all these scars happen to a child? how could the God that everyone covets let these things happen? How could anyone or anything let my mom die? One thing I can say is the memories are coming more. Or maybe I am just brooding more; that's clearly a flaw of mine. These memories, the glimpses as they come, I just don't know.

Ryder lifted his head, his gaze taking in the neatly furnished bath and the cats looking at him from a multitude of surfaces. He shifted and stood, beginning his daily routine before bed, talking to the cats as he did so, sadness in his voice.

"I am trying to find out the truth, and I'm just not sure if it will be the best thing. However, I just want, I want to know. You know, Aspasia, I just want the truth. I want to remember more than the smell of cinnamon and bright colors and blonde hair and blue eyes. I want to remember more than the few pictures I have sitting on my shelf, the few pictures that take up the mantle. I want to know my mom, the truth about what happened to her, and what, what happened to me. And I want to know why when I look at people. I know them, but I can't figure out why."

He rubbed the two cats' heads he hadn't said hello to, whispering softly to Diana and Willow. Smiling at Their identical pink noses and gray fur. "I just don't know, girls. You wouldn't know, but it is so frustrating to just get glimpses of bright things and graceful music and the cold hard steel on my cheek."

He started the bath, the water growing hotter and steam curling about the mirror. "I'm serious, you two. It's just awful to wake up in a hospital and having them tell me: a man gone bad, he stole my mother, my memories, and my good looks. That's why we had to come back."

He nodded at the two female cats as they walked around the shelves above the toilet. "I need to know the answers. I must."

He sighed, finished grumbling and hopped into the shower, letting the hot water sluice over the dull ache in his shoulders. Tomorrow was a new day for answers and for early morning questions. Besides, he was tired. Too many emotions in one day.

Ryder slid into silk sheets, the warm fur bodies on either side of his bed. Aristotle took up his own residence beside Ryder's head. Ryder smiled as he fell asleep; it never took him long to fall to sleep, and most cases it was dreamless.

However, as it had been lately, the dreams began. They plagued him with their twisted and strange meanings and their surreal quality, Ever since he had first came home.

Ryder stood along a forest canopy, the tree line large and encompassing. The tunic and breeches he wore would have been home to a hunter or peasant in bygone days in Shakespearian plays. At first, he stood dumbfounded, trying to make sense of where he was and what was going on, while slowly coming to the realization that he was dreaming, but it was not possible to wake up yet. His mind slowly began to latch onto the thought at hand, the mission of sorts that he was on, but what it was he didn't know. He stared in confusion at the bright colors that shot along the forest treetops, and the smell of cinnamon that wafted toward him had him running toward it. Ryder stopped short to stare at the wings

that hung suspended in the air, big enough for a man his size. Their black color was a startling contrast to the white band that wore its way around their middle, breaking up the obsidian. He reached forward to trace the line that wove around and stopped his hand held aloft in midair. A loud roar reached his ears. He looked about him, his body trembling, waiting for some beast, but as he listened closer, it was not a creature, just a multitude of voices screaming the words "You failed" over and over again.

Ryder looked back to the wings, a familiar ache beginning in his chest, one from earlier in the library. Ryder threw himself forward as the sound of a woman crying drew him closer and closer to the fathomless shadows that took up space between the trees. The woman that kneeled in the shadows turned to look at him, but her face was blank. He screamed and threw himself backward as her face began to materialize and then morph to others, others he knew but didn't. He screamed at the sky.

"What is this torture?" He turned and ran from the woman in the woods toward the bright lights, but his steps were sluggish and slow. As he finally made it, he closed his eyes as the world fell away beneath his feet. He was falling to his death, he was certain of it.

Ryder woke with a gasp and stared around his room. He gasped, his chest tight, breathing labored, each breath agony and sweat poured down his face. There was a heavy lump on his chest, and he choked on a laugh when he realized it was Aristotle doing his best to make him feel better.

"That was a terrible dream," he spoke to the four set of cat eyes that stared up at him. "Logically, I know it was a dream, a terrible, crazy dream. But it felt so real."

He looked to the clock on his brown bedside table and shook his head at the 5:00 am that blinked at him. He pulled the blankets from his sweaty chest and went straight toward the bathroom. A quick wash down, some coffee and a jog. That was what he needed right now, some control in his off-kilter head.

CHAPTER 5

XERA

Xera woke with a soft gasp and sat up, tears streaming down her face at the pain in her leg. She trembled as she pushed herself to the edge of the bed. Reaching into the nightstand for her water bottle and the pills that chased away the pain, she swallowed them quick, shuddering at their foul taste. She pulled her robe around her shoulders and hobbled toward the window and the gray morning outside. She settled in her chair and waited for the sunrise, hoping it would wipe away the darkness of the morning. Good days always came with sunrises.

Xera rubbed her eyes, trying to force them open and herself awake. The tear stains on her cheek were cold in the air conditioned room. Shifting, she stretched and sighed. She had not had a restful evening. Her thoughts were full of dreams that made no sense. The sounds of crying and bright lights. There was also darkness and evil things, but they were fast fading from her mind.

It's probably just my medicine; pain medication always makes me so agitated and strange. I wish I didn't have to take it, but the walks from class to class are hard on my healing leg. Curse my stepfather and his idiocy. I never would have had to lose my mother or take pain pills so much if it wasn't for him.

Xera crossed her arms and shook her head, more upset with her own demons and how they affected her than anything else. She looked around and spoke to the empty room.

"I just need to stop letting it affect me so. Mother always told me to keep a stiff upper lip, so I will. But my goodness, I am so tired of these onslaughts of pain."

Xera leaned back into her chair and let her mind wander to the sleepless night she had. So many things, fires and loud whispers and running. She had done so much running in her sleep. Xera shook her head, a rueful smile on her face.

Why am I even worried about these nightmares? I always have nightmares with pain medication. It's the normal for me. It doesn't matter that these things felt different. I am just stressed out, that is all. Mom's birthday is coming up and everything is so new. I am just a little stretched thin.

A nice cup of warm tea will sort me right out.

Xera groused to herself and began to push herself from her chair when a movement from outside caught her line of sight. Turning, she studied the form of the man jogging and felt her cheeks heat when she realized it was the librarian. She shook her head and smiled to herself.

"Oh am I glad he can't see me. As if I didn't make a big enough fool of myself yesterday at the library. Mooning about and staring at him as I did."

It's not like anyone could blame me, though. I may not have had many boyfriends, but I can certainly appreciate a good-looking man. And he is gorgeous with that black hair and those mocha brown eyes. And the solid body he held, there was sheer power to him. Honestly, it was scary, but not in a bad way. Perhaps he is the one thing to lift my spirits on this dreary day.

Xera smiled to herself and snuck another look out her window. The muscles that made up his shoulders were strong and chorded. She blushed again, and she couldn't take her eyes from him. As she continued to study him in more detail from the secrecy of her own haven, a light fell upon his back. As it spilled across his chiseled shoulders, she exhaled sharply, but she gasped when his back was completely bared to her. She covered her mouth in horror. His back was covered in scars, and two very long, ropy scars went from the middle of his shoulders and further down to right before his pants.

It was awful.

Oh my goodness. How terrible, look at those scars. What on earth happened to him? No wonder he was so sensitive about his face when I accidentally gasped. He was used as someone's cutting board. Who would do that to another person? For that matter, why would they do it?

Xera took a brief moment to look down at her own scarred knee, to trace her fingers along the seam of the incision that had put her shattered knee back together. All of a sudden, her dreary day didn't seem all that terrible. She was healed; she had worked hard to get to where she was, to walk again. He would have to have spent much longer in the hospital than she for his grievous wounds. She squeezed her knee and returned her gaze to the fading shadow of the man as he ran back toward the campus.

He stopped once and he turned. He looked at her window and Xera leaned to the side. However, he shook his head and continued on. An irritating burning began in her chest, and she shook her head. It was time for some tea and then she must start her day. And depressing thoughts about her life and the scars that covered the librarian's back had no place in it.

Chapter 6

Duff

Duff stood in the early morning shadows, and in his arms, stirring, was the woman he had fallen in love with. She nipped at his shoulder as she leaned into him, her hair falling around her face and her cool blue eyes gazing up at him. He looked down at her. So similar to another, yet so different. He would have never thought such a creature as he could feel this way. However, she had weaved a spell around him, had ensnared his senses, and there was no going back, not now. She had bound him fully his heart, his soul, they belonged to her. If he even had one of each; some days he wasn't so sure. He shifted and mused on how much of a hold she had on him, so tightly, in fact, it frightened him on a good day. She made his thoughts tender toward her. Well, as caring as he could allow.

He shifted, moving her from the circle of his arms. "Tamesis, are you sure this is what you want to do? And for that matter, do you need to do this? Why can't it just be some other woman's soul? She is watched over by two guardians, two."

Tamesis looked up at him again, her blue eyes boring into him. She simpered cruelly. "Are you scared of a big bad guardian, Duff? A guardian who doesn't even realize he is one? Honestly, and yes," she snapped at him and whirled away, crossing her arms.

Duff growled at the warmth she had taken, the cool morning air seeping into the spot she had been leaning against. She stared at him, her eyes crackling at him.

"Of course it has to be her, Duff. She needs to give me her soul. I told you, the seer has spoken. She owes me something, and she will give it to me! I had to watch for years as she was given everything. Not anymore. I won't allow her to have one more thing."

Duff growled again and waved a hand in her face. "The seer has spoken. Do you hear yourself, Tam? I am strong, you know this, but even I don't know if I could handle both guardians. They are strong, have years of power to wield. And if the one, if he realizes it. No matter what I do, I can't save you. I have fought with him before yes, but it was always a fight to the death and he has killed me near as many times as I have killed him."

He snorted. "And the seer, the precious soothsayer gets her rocks off by toying with people. She speaks in riddles and rhymes, often leading those who listen to their deaths. Not to mention, Tam, she belongs to my mother. My mother owns her Seer. You both could be wrong. And the girl doesn't even know who you are, Tam! She has no memories. And she wouldn't have them of you anyway. Compared to her, you are eons younger even if you were born at the same time in the here and now."

Duff cringed as she smiled, all sharp teeth and bright red lips. A grin of pure evil. His heart rate quickened and his breathing too. He winced, knowing what was coming, and she struck.

She grabbed his upper arms, digging her bright red nails into his flesh. He should have known. She loved to inflict pain, his Tamesis, loved to hurt those around her. And she always, always attacked after she grinned. Duff Frowned at her obvious lack of judgment. She was so anxious to gain her immortality that she couldn't wait for the normal ways. No, she had to do some task, make someone give up their soul for her immortal gain, and for some reason, she was fixated on just one woman to make it happen.

"Tamesis, I am even stronger than you and even I don't know if I could end the girl with the Angel's blessing. This could, probably will, end badly."

Tamesis curled her lip, digging further into his skin. "Shut up, you dog. You will do what I say if you love me as you say you do. You will get the girl for me, and I will end her."

Duff looked to her and then down and he nodded, knowing it was futile to talk his mate out of this horrifying mess. He flexed his hand, the dark shadow infused blood sliding down his ash-laden skin. Tamesis retracted her claws and giggled girlishly, peppering his cheeks with kisses.

"See, I knew you would agree."

She smoothed her hands along his dark chest, glancing up at him through her eyelashes. Duff couldn't stop the smile from gracing his devilish face at her bedroom eyes.

"Must you put your glamor on so soon? You like yourself so much better in this form; I like you so much better in this form."

Duff snarled and shook his head. How he hated blending in with the mortal realm, walking among the fleshy bags of blood and emotions. Ugh, it wasn't fair.

"Soon it will be like it was in bygone years, Tam. You'll see. Soon, I will walk among the humans as I did before, as what I am. None of this constant changing and shrinking and adding." He reached up to scratch one of his horns.

Tamesis giggled again, high and girlish. "Oh

yes, when we do as the seer has commanded, we will take back the glory of the underworld. The seer said I would succeed, she told me I would make this work. Besides, that girl, she's just a mortal with a fancy blessing. Blessings, just like curses, can be broken. You'll see."

Duff stared at her and though he wanted to shake her, instead, he swung his hand in an arc and watched as a nearby car caught fire. He was getting irritated.

What he couldn't tell Tamesis was that the seer often would make up the outcome of her visions. Only she herself could see so far. She was in the business of pleasing people while lining her own pockets. It was a shame, really. And he knew Tamesis wouldn't do her own thinking. She was beautiful but not as smart as his mother or the other cosmic beings that roamed the heavens and nethers. She needed more years on her. There was more going on than even he or she knew.

Tamesis purred and rubbed against him. "So powerful."

He looked at her in disgust and shoved her away. He had enough of this whole situation and his mate right now. Besides, he had to get to his stupid class and act like he cared. Try and get a little mortal to trust him. Tamesis smiled at his roughness and blew him a kiss. Her red lips pulled in a sexy pout. This woman was going to be the death of him.

He knew it, but he could not turn it off no

matter how hard he tried. She was like a compulsion and an obsession. One that he was slowly starting to unravel. He turned away and started toward the building. He conjured a backpack out of thin air and tossed it over his shoulder. His large, lumbering steps took him swiftly toward the classroom. Only to stop as he saw the dark one jogging. A grim smile took its place across his face. He snorted and gave a small wave. He watched as Ryder stumbled on a rock and almost fell. He laughed to himself, immediately in a better mood than he had been in.

Chapter 7

Gideon

Gideon stood staring down at the young guardian as he jogged along the flagged stone path. His eyes sought out the young woman that watched from the shadowy eave of her window, and he smiled. Such a sweet girl, Xera was, always had been. It was too bad that, much like Ryder, she could remember nothing. Gideon scratched his head and moved away from the edge as someone materialized beside him.

He turned to look at the scarred man that hid further into the shadows. "Hello, Kavi."

"Good evening, Gideon. Your reflexes are beginning to wane, old man," he replied with a small sideways smirk.

A man with a face of torn flesh and a scarred throat stepped forward. The man spoke, his voice raspy and full of strangeness, as if it pained him to do so.

"How comes my son, Gideon? Has he begun to question yet?"

Kavi himself moved to the edge, and he stared down at the young man, sadness on his face.

"Such a troubled life he has had. I supposed it's my fault for listening to the lure of a pretty tongue. And my sweet little bride's fault for not giving up on me." The last part was said with half a smile, his face tilted at a strange angle.

Gideon stepped near him and looked down as well, touching the man's shoulder. "Oh Kavi, it is no one's fault really. Everything that comes to pass is meant to be. It is fate, destiny. They're fickle sisters you know. It's the Greek in them."

Kavi gave a strangled laugh as if the sound could not quite make it through his voice box. Gideon gave a slow, sad smile.

"And if we want to lay blame, even I could take some, my dear friend. I am old, Kavi, very old, perhaps I forgot a lesson. Perhaps I did not do my job of guiding and teaching as well as I could. I did not do my best."

Kavi shifted and looked to Gideon, his brown eyes piercing the other man's.

"You did your best, old friend. You always do. Ryder is a better man than me, and for that, you hold much of the credit for."

Gideon's cheeks heated at the praise. He shook his head and moved his hand. He stared down at the ink and the grime that covered them, the black edges of his fingers.

"Thank you for that, old friend. But no, Kavi, he has not started to question yet. I fear for him. This is his last chance, and I do not know if he is ready. I removed the papers from their resting place, so hopefully, he will start to notice them, or Xera will. She is smarter than most give her credit for. And I think this time she will succeed in beautiful ways."

"What will papers tell him, Gideon? He will find the answers to what happened to his mother this time, that is all. It will give him more questions that he needs to find the answers for and before we know it, the time will be upon us. And he will be ill-prepared again. This is his last chance or we lose him forever. And what he needs to know, what he needs to let happen, cannot be found in yellowing papers."

Gideon sighed and stretched. "I know it doesn't seem a lot, but you know as well as I that we cannot tell him anything. That he must figure it out on his own. If we get his brain working, make him question, he will come to the answers. He always does."

Gideon stroked his chin, thinking about the youth below him. If he could give little hints, to not give the major stuff away. Break the rules and Ryder figured it out. He didn't have to reveal his cosmic place in all of it. Besides, he frowned, he was beginning to worry about Ryder.

There was still so much that had to be revealed to the young man. Still so much for him to learn before he could ask the questions he really wanted to know. However, Ryder was beginning to question before he got the whole picture. And Gideon was unsure if it would close his eyes or close his heart or both, and it scared him. He would be lying if he said that Ryder wasn't one of his favorite students throughout the years.

Kavi sighed and nodded his grizzled head. "I know that, Gideon, but it doesn't make it any easier, especially as the time shrinks and he's no closer and this is his last chance. A father always worries, Gideon, believe me. And it is very unfair of the council to make us mute on it."

The other man squeezed Gideon's shoulder, and Gideon watched as he disappeared into the surrounding shadows. His shoulders drooped, and he wiped his eye.

I am getting too old for all of this. So glad this is my last mission. I just hope it has a happy ending.

Gideon sat at his desk, staring broodingly at the wall of books that made up his office. One quick glance and he took in the messy tabletops, the small apartment door that attached to his office open wide, and the mess from inside spilling out. However, he could no more lift a finger if he wanted to. His conversation with Kavi earlier had ruined his outlook for the day, bringing many of his own fears and worries to light. He could not blame Kavi for worrying as he did, for Ryder did not ask for any of this. It was not his fault that he was both blessed and cursed with the blessing.

Gideon stared at the interlocking letters that spelled the last name Greer on the leather-bound book in front of him. He touched it and sighed. It held all the secrets of those he had guarded with the last name of Greer. All those he had lost, when they gave into the curse that blessed them. To change the inside of a person, a mortal it had such terrible consequences. Yes, it made them stronger, faster, braver. Strong enough and more to protect the angels that walked the earth. However, without balance it could not exist. So they were cursed too. Always to fall in love with their mark. A sin that killed most of them, turned them into fallen's just as Ryder, and Kavi. Some could rise above after proving themselves of such trials, but most were lost. He rubbed his eyes and lifted the book to place in the drawer that locked.

Gideon tapped his fingers on the desk and stared at the wall of books and scrolls again. He growled to himself and crossed his arms.

Thousands of years of knowledge trapped in here. I have books that would their secrets come to light, the world would crumble. And I am unable to save one man and woman. They need to save themselves for crimes of their pasts. How is that fair? It's not. Rules they could not help but break, especially when fate involved herself, as she so often does. What a busybody.

Gideon paused his musings to listen as the foyer door opened. He strained his eyes to look past the frosted glass into the hallway beyond, and he gave a small smile at the form of Ryder, no longer jogging, but ready to begin his day. Gideon stood slowly and walked to the door, taking a moment to watch the young man.

Ryder took a deep breath of the parchment air, and Gideon clapped his hands quietly together, happy to see the true love of books and knowledge on the man's face. A man after his own heart, but his thoughts scattered and his smile faded as Ryder himself lost his elating glow and instead gave a harrowed and frowning look to the office door. Gideon shifted and lowered his eyes as Ryder hurried toward his office door, his boots resounding and echoing throughout the hall. One knock was all he needed. Gideon pasted a smile on his face and answered the door.

"Ryder, my dear boy. Did you enjoy your first day? But alas, young man, you look perturbed. I hope no one has upset you?"

The youthful man smiled to Gideon, and the old man had to take a quick breath. So blown away by the smile that looked so much like the young man's mother, it touched Gideon every time.

How I miss Trinity. Such a sweet, dear thing. She was a good mother, a good friend. I will see her again. I hope Ryder has not tired of his search already. He has been searching for years, going around in circles. The information lost to him. His self-conscious must be weary; mine would be. It is truly a shame that I can tell him nothing. The wisdom I could offer him.

Gideon had to stifle the smile that wanted to show at the smirk that slid along Ryder's face and the cheeky answer the young man gave him.

"No, no one has upset me. I don't think anyone would want too."

Gideon looked at the young man and smiled despite himself. "No, I don't suppose anyone would want to do that."

Gideon waited for the real reason Ryder was there. Ryder shifted and spoke.

"I know you know I lived here before, sir, and that I suffered certain tragedies as a child. I was just curious if it was against our policy to allow me to do my own research into some events of my past?"

Gideon gave a small smile, thankful that this was an answer he could give the boy. Something that didn't actually delve into his past. However, he wanted to tell the boy to proceed with caution. But how without giving away that he knew more than he acted as he did?

"It is not against our rules, no. And I, of course, have no objection to this. However, are you sure you want to delve into what could be a very painful reveal for you?"

Gideon waited for the inevitable lift of the young man's lip, the raised brow to show his confusion and curiosity. Just because Ryder had forgotten him did not mean he had forgotten Ryder. It was not long before he was rewarded with the usual fare.

Ryder spoke with authority he didn't quite have, but all the same, it resounded throughout the small area the two men stood in.

"I need the answers. I am sure. Why wouldn't I be?"

A soft pressure deep in Gideon's chest caused him pause, and he swallowed. He weighed his words carefully before answering. His warm brown eyes met the darker ones of the youth, and he spoke softly. "I simply meant this will be a painful ordeal. I remember the news coverage, and it was not pretty. And, well, they never caught the man. I would not want you to dwell on him. I know that you did not have an easy go of it after that. It will be difficult, and I just fear that it could interfere with your everyday life."

Ryder's jaw tightened, and he backed up a step, his nostrils flaring. Gideon watched with bemusement as the young man forced himself to calm down, taking deep breaths. So hot headed the young Ryder, always had been. At least he had learned to control it, most of the time.

The youth spoke. "You needn't worry about that. I won't let it affect my everyday life, nor my job."

Gideon nodded his head with slow movements. "Then I see nothing wrong with it. If you should need some help, please don't hesitate to ask."

Ryder shifted and dipped his head with a softly murmured "Thank you."

And walked away back to his desk. Gideon watched him go, his heart feeling heavier than it had that morning. He reached out but stopped. He wanted to check on the boy's well-being, to ask him if he was getting sleep or if the dreams had started. If he was anxious because they made no sense. However, Gideon sighed and mentally cursed. He was unable to ask any of that, as that would give away his position in this large event.

No interfering. I wish I had never agreed to that, but I needed to watch him. It is what I do; I am his guardian. I must teach him, guide him, and those above me are making it near impossible. So glad this is my last mission. I am getting far too old for this.

Gideon stared at the youth as he busied himself at his desk, the droop of his shoulders, the dark circles under his eyes, and he sighed, sadness weighing heavy on his form.

Oh Trinity, my dear, sweet girl. Why did you have to fall in love with one fated to walk in both realms? Your son has been cursed because of it. Though it is no fault of his own or his parents really, they just followed fate, those fickle sisters always causing problems. And even I cannot imagine life without you or Kavi together as one.

Gideon turned away, grasping his own briefcase and with burdens heavier on his shoulders than moments before, he walked out the doors and to his first class of the day. Pausing only to wish the young librarian a good day.

Chapter 8

Xera

Xera traveled across the manicured lawn, in her arms the books for her classes and on top, the journal of all her strange dreams. She shifted but couldn't quite wipe the darkness of the night before pervading her senses. The awful dreams of blood and darkness and feathers, strange feathers. She shivered in the sunlight, tucking her arms tighter around her books, a sharp sense of foreboding stealing her breath away. She stopped moving to look all around, the hair on the back of her neck standing up again.

He's in jail, Xera; he is locked up. He can't hurt you anymore, and he definitely can't hurt Mom anymore, bless her soul. I don't know why I am so jumpy. Everything feels so strange. Like, like something is going to happen sometime soon, something really bad. Ugh, nonsense, Xera, you are being foolish again, your imagination going wild. You put too much stock in superstitions and gut feelings.

Xera rubbed her leg, blinking at the quickly fading sunlight. She looked up to catch the first drop of rain on her nose. She sighed and squeezed the knee between finger and thumb. She'd never make it on a run, not today. No wonder her knee hurt, always bothering her in the nasty weather. And it was clear that rain was coming, though she hadn't remembered reading it on the forecast.

Sometimes I wish I was whole. I should not have to spend my twenties in constant pain. It just isn't fair. It's all his fault, him and his stupid addictions. I told Mom she needed to get away, told her he was going to kill us all. Now look. I'm an orphan again.

Xera frowned and shook her head, trying to dispel the depressing thoughts. Thoughts that lay on her like a melancholy blanket of darkness. She continued walking, keeping her head down, going through the items she needed to do today.

I imagine part of my problem is that it is Mom's birthday, so perhaps I need to figure out something to do in honor of her? Maybe that will make my day better. But what? It has been so long since I celebrated, too many months of therapy and surgeries. I didn't have the time.

Xera smiled to herself, remembering this day over fourteen years ago when she sat down to celebrate her foster mother's birthday and to find that she was the one getting the gift that day. She was the one who, at ten years old, was finally finding the home she had always longed for. They had a day out for breakfast and then the rest of the day was spent at the bookstores reminiscing and hunting for that perfect book.

That's what I'll do. I can't go to a bookstore today, but perhaps the library. Maybe I can just take the last period that I have nothing to do and just read. I am sure the library is nice and cozy, and if not, I can always take some books home to my own little sitting room.

She looked to the blackening sky again and shook her head. It was indeed one of the perfect days to sit and read. She was surprised out of her memories and thoughts by the man stomping toward her. She lifted her hand to wave but was thrown off balance when Duff kept going past her, not even returning her wave. She was momentarily surprised, but he looked back at her and nodded his head. Dark thunder clouds in his eyes.

"Sorry, Xera. Now is not a good time. I forgot my backpack. I'll see you in class."

Xera closed her mouth as she has been about to speak and instead nodded and held her head down as she pushed onward to class and warmth. Her thoughts were on the reprieve she would have that evening. And if she was honest, the man that ran the library.

CHAPTER 9

TAMESIS

The other woman stood in the shadows of the nearby tea shop, holding a cigarette between her forefinger and thumb, a fixed snarl on her face. She growled under her breath and watched in revulsion as the disgusting little tart waved at her Duff like she owned him.

"He belongs to me, you little whore. He is mine. He belongs to me, yet another thing for you to pay for. He doesn't belong to you. It is all a ruse. He doesn't care for you; you are not friends," she muttered under her breath, lifting her lip in a sneer at the people nearby that stared at her.

I'll make her pay. I'll make her wish she had never been born. I'll rip her to shreds. I'll ruin her. I will kill her. She steals everything!

Tamesis growled and stomped away, her small hands held tight at her side while she mused. People moved from her space without a backward glance. She slid into a nearby alley to pace to and fro without bother. She sniffed once and wrinkled her nose as decaying leaves and sulfur invaded her senses. She stood motionless, sweat sliding down her back. She hurriedly looked around, fear tearing at her insides. She grasped her stomach, while it rolled and frothed.

The smell was intoxicating to her senses, and it caused a strange warmth to gather in all her extremities and insides. She knew who it belonged to, and it caused her stomach to tighten. Her heart stopped when the beautiful woman materialized in front of her. She was encased in layers of black leather, form fitting enough to leave nothing to the imagination. Her hair fell around her waist in a long, shimmering length of obsidian, and around her hips, she wore two black whips, and spiked jewelry covered her arms and neck. Tamesis shuddered under the heaviness of her black-eyed, long-lashed gaze. She sneered at her with lips of rose red, and Tamesis was forced to her knees by a cosmic pressure behind her back. The woman laughed low and melodious, dark and mysterious as she moved closer to Tamesis, her pointed, black boots shaking the ground.

Tamesis sighed in quiet, forceful pleasure as the woman drew near her and traced her fingers along her cheek, leaving warmth and heaviness in her wake. Tamesis fought the feeling to lean into the woman's hand, but it was futile, and she whimpered as she pulled her hand away.

"Tamesis Jade, so jealous. It's so unbecoming. Have I not told you that Duff cannot stray, that he will not stray? Yet you still worry about it, you fool. There are much more important things to worry about, you stupid woman. And it should not matter if he would; you will still get the girl's death in the end, and that is the true prize."

The woman neared her running her fingers further along Tamesis's back, causing goose flesh to break out in its wake. She bent to Tamesis ear and spoke sharply. "Stand up, girl!"

The last command was like a bull whip; it lashed across Tamesis's conscious and forced her to her feet. She moved so quick she stumbled and fell at the other woman's feet, only to scrabble and fight to get back up. The leather-clad woman laughed, the sound, cruel and haughty.

"At least you make me laugh, silly girl. So few have that ability."

Tamesis's faced heated up and burning pain circled in the pit of her stomach at the haughty voice and irritating way the woman spoke down to her. Tamesis's eyes went wide as she grasped her own throat, it was burning and she was choking. She wanted to scream as her throat began to close. The woman drew near, grasping her shoulder and pulling her into her circle of arms. Warmth pooled deep into Tamesis's center and her eyes dilated as she met the gaze of the dark queen.

"You never disrespect me, child. I can end you just as easily as I made you. You are nothing, no one, without my son and myself, do you hear me? You owe Lilith your life. You are a daughter of darkness and you should act as such."

Lilith dropped her from her arms, and Tamesis again fell to her knees, gasping, tears streaming down her face and her knees smarting from the fall. Lilith walked around her, the sharp sound of her booted heels loud in the alleyway.

"I said stand up, girl!" The command was given quietly and deadly. Tamesis struggled to her feet, her face wet with snot and tears. She sniffled and tried to calm the tremors that still wracked her body as well as the red haze of lust in her eyes.

"Ugh, stop sniveling, stupid harlot. And stand still. How hard is it to stand up? Fool." Lilith curled her lip at her and wrinkled her nose.

Tamesis struggled to stay upright, to calm her roaring emotions, to steal her back, but she was fast losing the battle. The queen of sin, Lilith herself whose most prominent sin was disobedience tempered lust. She beckoned Tamesis like a siren song, but the girl could do nothing, no control of her own actions.

The older woman continued to walk around oblivious to the girl's struggle. "Having second thoughts, are you, Tamesis? You say you want power, so even out of the goodness of my heart, I take you to meet my Seer. To ask her what you must do, and here you are shirking your duty. You have not found a place for the ritual, and even now I have my creatures scouring, searching for Cain's dagger. Something you should have found." The woman stopped moving to stare at Tamesis.

Tamesis tightened her jaw, the tears still streaming down her face at the fact that she was literally frozen in place and could do nothing but listen.

"Oh so many waterworks, girl. The Seer told you, you would get to kill the girl, but you need to gain her trust first. Seeing as how we have to do things differently this time. The Greer, however, is mine; you know this. Yet you plot his demise as well. Such a need to destroy this girl. So, close minded. There is more at stake here Tamesis. More than just your little spat with her."

The woman looked her over in distaste. A bitter taste burned the back of Tamesis's throat, and she quickly averted her gaze, the only thing she could do. "Well. Seeing that you can't get her trust. Duff will need to, and you will let him. None of this temper tantrum fit throwing; it is very unbecoming. You will wait for the thousandth day of the thousandth year. And you will do nothing but wait. And if Duff cannot gain her trust, which he probably won't since it's Duff. He's an idiot, then I have another plan in place, but you still must wait. You stupid girl."

Lilith cradled Tamesis's face in the palm of her hand, sliding it down along to her chin.

"And Tamesis, I mean that. Do not disappoint me. I am the queen of the damned, and I can do things to you that you can't even imagine especially if I am displeased. There are bigger things at work than your immortality; that is just an added bonus, I suppose. Though I don't know how I'll handle you forever. Remember, Tamesis Jade, you do nothing. I made you, I own you, I can and will destroy you should you disobey."

The woman turned away, and Tamesis watched as she swirled away in a whirlwind of scattered shadows and the smell of decaying leaves. Tamesis felt the magic lessen and again she fell to her knees. Repressed sobs wracked her body as she curled into a ball in the filth of the alley. She had promised herself she would never allow someone to hold such power over her, but the queen held so much over her. Tamesis covered her face with her filthy hands and cried, rocking back and forth. As the tears ran dry and the sobs grew quiet, Tamesis pushed to her feet and she stumbled home, anxious for a bath, a bed, and Duff. And she promised herself no more tears.

CHAPTER 10

XERA

Xera shook her long hair from the back of her neck. She stared in dismay at the sheets of rain that fell from the heavens to wet the ground. She shuddered and pulled her blanket tighter around her body. She couldn't quite get the chill from her bones. Which surprised her as it was not a cold rain, just a wet one. She stared at the pile of wet laundry sitting on the floor, waiting for her to remove it. She shook her head and walked back to the window, staring out at the library only a few feet away, but it seemed like so far in the torrential downpour of rain.

She tilted her head, the window open just a crack for her to listen as it fell. She sniffed. At least it smelled good out there, clean, new, fresh. She needed that today, a new something, anything really. What she really wanted was to read a new book in the cozy library. To remember without pain her mother and their own reading adventures together.

I miss her so much. It's so unfair. How could God take her from me with so much violence? Why would he let such a terrible man live and a beautiful woman inside and out succumb to her injuries? It just wasn't fair.

Xera stomped her foot and cried out as she stepped on something sharp and pointed. She kneeled down, holding her bleeding foot and lifted the little silver necklace from the floor. She smiled gently at the open-faced book that stared up at her. The tiny message etched in the golden plating. *Journey to new worlds through words.*

Xera traced her fingers overtop of the small raised letters, tears sliding down her face, her mother had bought that for her on her eighteenth birthday. She slid the necklace around her neck and slowly limped toward the bathroom to take care of her foot.

This is just a beautiful ending to such a horrible day. No excuses if this wasn't a sign I don't know what is. I will go to that library rain be damned.

Xera slid from her warmly lit and dry cottage and stood on the porch staring at the library and the rain as it came down in torrents. She jumped from the porch, her leg hurting, but determined, she ran toward the large double doors. Her long hair flew behind her and as she made it to the library doors, she stood panting at first, trying to catch her breath before she entered the sanctuary of books.

She looked through the windows and saw the librarian Ryder sitting at his tiny desk. The thunder clapped behind her, making her jump, and she shoved the doors open as lightning crackled across the sky and lit up the small entryway, the shadowy eaves and the face of the librarian. A beam traced his face and outlined the scar that he wore like a king. She followed the path, wondering not for the first time what terrible things had happened to him and what he had seen.

She was startled from her thoughts by the feel of hot breath on the back of her neck, and she jumped out of the way as Duff stood there glaring at both her and the librarian through hazel eyes. She covered her mouth at his disheveled appearance. His usually perfectly coiffed hair was bedraggled, and the clothes that he already wore too tight were soaking wet and squeezing him. She was certain he wouldn't be able to breathe right.

"I'm sorry, Duff. I didn't see you. I hope you weren't waiting long."

The man sneered and nodded his head. "I know. You ran right past me and then stopped right in front of me so I couldn't get in. But please, by all means, continue to stare at our librarian while my back gets soaked. It's so kind of you."

Xera blushed and jumped forward, anxious to give him the room he needed to get in and the space he clearly needed to calm himself down.

"I said I was sorry. It's pouring buckets out there, what do you expect? I didn't know you were there."

Duff tightened his jaw and shook his head. "Just pay attention next time, Xera. You're always running around with your head in the clouds. You know, there's some of us here on earth that would like a little attention too. You know, your friends?"

Xera stared at him in surprise, her blush deepening. "What in the world, Duff? What has gotten into you?"

Before she could say more, someone touched her shoulder from behind. She froze as a strange sensation sizzled up her spine and deep into her back. It was like lightning, vibrant and alive resounding within. She squeezed her palms together, their sudden clamminess unnerving. The librarian stepped in front of her, his jawline tight and his eyes dark and menacing.

"That is no way to talk to anyone. Especially not a lady. What gives you the right to even open your mouth with such cold intent? She said she didn't see you, and that should be the end of it."

Duff snorted and stared at the librarian, his eyes

shooting heat. Xera backed up a step, her fingers shaking, but she wasn't certain if it was from the wet rain or the anxiousness that skittered along her body.

"I wasn't talking to you. I was talking to my friend. Perhaps you should stay out of it. She is an adult."

Xera raised her hand, opening her mouth to speak when the librarian spoke, his voice low in timbre and vibrating with barely concealed anger.

"None of my business? For starters, Duff, I believe I heard the young lady call you before, you are in the library of which I am the librarian, so yes, it is my business. Secondly, if you are going to air your dirty laundry for the whole world to hear, then I can say whatever I want. And you are being downright rude. Sometimes people just don't see people, especially in that. Have you looked outside, you idiot? It is pouring buckets."

As the two squared off, Xera looked around, hoping that someone would be near. Seeing no one, she sighed and straightened her back. She stepped between the two and placed a hand on each, though with both she had to almost stand on tiptoes. She cleared her throat and stared at one then the other.

"This is ridiculous, both of you." She turned to Duff. "I am sorry, Duff. I did not see you. I know sometimes I can be a bit, well, air headed."

The man snorted, and she lowered her

eyebrows. "However, that does not give you any right to treat me so abhorrently. Especially given that you know how I feel about that type of behavior anyway. So, Ryder is right on that aspect."

She turned back to the librarian, and her face softened as she traced the contours of his face with her eyes "Thank you for standing up for me, but I am a big girl."

When she met his eyes, they were dark and serious, troubled even. He frowned in thought and growled as he held out his hand to Duff. "Truce for now. But I hear it again and I will kick you out. Regardless of whether or not Miss Xera protests. Now, may I please ask what you two are doing in the foyer dripping rainwater everywhere?"

Xera watched as he pulled his hand back after Duff had not shaken it and crossed his arms, the muscles of his biceps tightening and making her eyes grow wide. She forced herself to look away, eyes training onto a piece of paper written on his desk with dates and figures, and it made her head swim with the sheer amount of tiny writing on it. She shook her head as the dates buzzed behind her eyes, and she rubbed them.

It has been a long day. I think I just need to find a book and go home and relax. Perhaps this gnawing headache will go away.

She shuddered in the silence and spoke, filling the uncomfortable quietness that pervaded all around her. Especially as the two alpha males in front of her sized each other up.

"I'm sorry that we got off on the wrong foot today. I just, well, I just wanted to check some books out. I finished Jane Eyre again. I didn't look at the hours. I hope we aren't intruding on your closing time. Or if you close for bad weather."

Xera shifted from foot to foot, pulling at her shirt as it stuck to her uncomfortably. She was ready to get out of her wet clothes and settle down to read.

Ryder gave her a half smile and dipped his head. "No, I'm here for a little bit yet. Please help yourselves. Remember, Duff, no fighting in the library."

The librarian gave one last reminder and shambled off toward his desk. Xera let out the breath she hadn't realized she was holding and shook her head.

She turned to meet the darkened eyes of Duff. He spoke through a mouth of ice. "I really don't like that guy. Who's he to tell me how I can speak to anybody?"

Xera gasped and crossed her arms. "Really, Duff! You were really mean, and I apologized. I don't understand why you're so bent out of shape anyway. Come on already. And besides, he is right, he is the librarian. So, his word is law, at least in here."

Duff shrugged and kicked at the ground. Xera

snorted. He looked like a spoiled child.

Honestly, if our parents weren't friends and I had more than just him to talk to, he and I would not associate this much. Ugh. Sometimes I wish I wasn't such a loner. I need more friends. I deserve to be treated better. I honestly just don't understand how his mother was my mother's best friend. Ugh.

She looked at him, and her body softened as he looked down. "I'm sorry." He rubbed the back of his neck. "You know, I just got in this fight with my girlfriend, and I just guess I needed a friend is all."

Xera's eyes went wide, and she gave him a soft smile. "I didn't even know you had a girlfriend. I'm sorry you fought. Do you want to find some books with me or talk about it?"

Duff shook his head. "Naw, books aren't my thing, and I hate talking about feelings. I'm going to go catch up with the girlfriend. See you later, Xera."

Xera watched him go back into the rain, a small wave of guilt chasing itself up her spine and deep into her chest.

He had no right to treat me that way, but, well, I guess I can forgive him this time. His girlfriend and him were fighting after all.

Xera shook her head and crossed her arms. She hugged herself, trying to warm up her arms and body.

Xera jumped when a voice spoke from her left.

"You know he had no right to talk to you that way? I don't know why you let him get away with it. Even if he fought with someone."

Xera met the gaze of the librarian again and smiled. "You don't know Duff like I do. He's, well, he's different. He's spoiled, but he means no harm. And besides, he said he had a fight with his girlfriend, and I imagine were I him, I would be cranky too."

Ryder shrugged. "Still not right to take it out on his friend. But here. You look cold." He held out a heavy green sweatshirt in front of her, the smell of man and Old Spice wafting toward her. Xera smiled as she took it. "But."

The librarian shook his head. "Nonsense. You keep it for now. Besides, it will probably look better on you than me anyway."

Ryder gave her a sideways smile and turned away. Xera watched him go and after he was out of sight, she pulled the sweatshirt over top of her head. It was ten times too big for her, but warmth sunk into her body and she smiled. Grabbing the nearby book she had been looking at, she walked happily toward the librarian's desk.

Xera turned the corner from the historical fiction section, and she froze at the sight that met her. Ryder sat back in his chair, his, denim-clad legs propped up on the desk and the worn out combat boots on his feet made her smile. Her mother had told her once that shoes were amazing and if they could just tell the story of the person that wore them, where they had been. Especially the most worn. He leaned there languid, a restless air taking up the silence between them. He was so relaxed, but she could see the tightly-coiled body ready to spring if need be.

What horrors he must have seen to be so on edge all the time. So rigid you can feel it in the air around him.

A tattoo played peekaboo with his shirt sleeve, and she wondered at it. It looked to be interlocking circles, but she really couldn't tell. She wondered if it were similar to the one that splashed across his back. He was so different than many of the librarians she had met. She felt him gazing at her through long eyelashes and a lock of hair fell down across his forehead, brushing the tips of his brows. Much like that of a child that you couldn't get their hair to stay straight. The scar that traced his face was white and stood out starkly against his tanned skin. He held a rugged bearing, but Xera was certain that vulnerability peeked at her from brown eyes if she could just find it. Or more if he would just show it, and then perhaps he wouldn't be so tense all the time.

There's something about him. I know him, but yet I don't know him. He's so familiar. I just can't shake it. I know him, but why?

She was thrown from her thoughts when he spoke. "Did you find everything you were looking for, Miss McCall?"

Xera smiled and held out the book, and he quickly checked it out. "Ah, that is a good one. I think you will enjoy it. Have a good night."

Xera smiled and slid out into the rain.

CHAPTER 11

RYDER

Ryder stepped through the familiar doors of his cottage and sighed. He stretched and moved, the tightness in his shoulders and the wet shirt that stuck to him making him uncomfortable. Ryder pulled at the shirt as he called out to his furry friend. He needed his little pal, a good soft cuddle, and to hash out the day's events, even if the cat didn't answer him back. It helped to organize his thoughts. And he and Aris, they had an unbreakable bond, the bond of two broken souls struggling to survive.

Gods, that woman! How could she let that idiot talk to her like he did and then justify it? Why can't I just write her off, just forget she exists? Ha, that's impossible, she's so damned beautiful she makes my head spin. And she's just so, so naïve and innocent.

I just want to take care of her. I really have to kick this problem. I can't save everyone, and I shouldn't try. Perhaps I am doomed to fulfill my mother's mistakes. Try and save all the strays and get hurt doing it. That much I do remember. Pretty sure some of these scars of mine are from that as well.

As his feline friend rushed to meet him, he gathered the tabby into his arms and sighed, momentarily forgetting the shirt that clung to him. He rubbed his cheek along the cat's downy fur. He shifted and stroked his fur as he walked toward the bathroom.

"Today was an interesting day, Aris. I almost got into a fight in the library of all places. That girl Xera came, you know, and so did that buffoon of hers that follows her around. You should have heard the way he spoke with her. It was awful. I should have just sunk my knuckles into his jaw. I don't think she knew how to take either one of us, and she tugged on her hair. It was rather cute honestly, but such a tell. Strange to see a tell on someone now."

Ryder rubbed his chin as he thought of the girl and the clear tell of abuse she had. The shy, naïve quality to herself. He laughed as the cat in his arms butted his cheek, stealing his attention.

"Okay, okay I'm sorry. I got lost in thought. I just wanted to take care of her and just wipe that filth right out of his mouth. He was so nasty. No one should ever talk to a woman as disrespectfully as that. And then she defended him. Why on earth would she do that? Clearly, it upset her, and she even gave him the devil a little bit."

He rubbed the cat's head harder, and the first purr broke the silence. "Yeah, I know you agree with me. At least someone does."

Ryder let the cat gently down to the ground as he continued traveling throughout the hallway, the cat at his heels. "He refused to shake my hand. Xera growled at me for being nice. Can you believe that? Anyway, what kind of person refuses a sign of good faith? He left soon after that. No man is a good man that can't look another in the eye or shake his hand. Makes 'em shifty."

Ryder looked down at his pals and patted their heads before he jumped into the shower. He leaned his head against the shower head, the waters sluicing down his back, and he sighed. He rubbed at his aching temples, cursing silently at the pain that exploded behind his eyelids. Another migraine, third one this week. And this one felt like it was going to be a doozy, possibly laying him up for days. He rubbed his eyes, his legs feeling shaky and weak, and he swallowed thickly at the coating of bile in his throat from the pain.

Ryder stepped from his bathroom, pulling the cinch waist pants tighter, and he made his way on tired muscles to the armchair in his living room. Falling into it, he sighed and rubbed at the white cat that settled on his chair with him. "Hello, Aspasia."

Ryder closed his eyes and rubbed absently at

the corded muscles bunched beneath the tattoo that took up the expanse of his right bicep. Restless circles around and around, soothing and calming. It pained him lately, and he wondered if after all these years he was growing allergic to the ink. He had it as long as he could remember. It had been brand new on his seventeenth birthday, and it was one of the few things he had thought about while recovering in the hospital. Why had he gotten it, and what did it mean? Three circles intertwined and linked. Over the years, he had added his own embellishments to its colors and the titles of his own careers, even adding colors and pretty designs.

Ryder looked down at the bushy gray tail that twitched at his feet and met the eyes of one of his Maine Coons. "Willow," he cooed at her, and the fat cat jumped into his lap and snuggled against his chest, laying her paw across his hand as he continued to rub his mark.

"You know, sweet girl, I don't ever remember any of these tattoos, not this one. Not the one on my back that says Guardian or any of the others. I am always in a dark place when I get them, always lost in my own thoughts. What kind of person does that make me? What type of animal or beast am I that I cannot remember a good bit of my life?"

He sighed and leaned his head into the plush green of the armchair and closed his eyes. Hoping that the sleep that tickled his eyelids would soothe the headache that pushed his pain tolerance.

CHAPTER 12

DUFF

Duff paced from one set of his hard-worn wooden floors to the other. His glamor was long gone, and the ash of his skin fell to land on the floor, leaving long, black marks the whole way from one end of his forming path to the other. He snarled to himself.

"I followed her like an idiot. I know better than to go into that library. Not only is Ryder freaking Greer there, but so is Gideon the righteous. I knew better, but Tamesis, she needs me to keep an eye on Xeraphina. It's achingly sad actually."

The creature stopped pacing and rubbed his chin, standing still in the dim light, thinking about the naïve little creature he was tasked with following. He looked around and spoke to the silence.

"There's no challenge. She just doesn't even get it. This hunt is losing its luster. I hate it; I am tired of it. I just want it to be over, all of it. The only thing new is this time, it is not for my mother that I hunt them like dogs, no, it is for Tamesis. My Soulless. It's time to retire. Too many centuries of doing this."

He shook his head and snorted. Today of all days he had followed her into a library. Why anyone would want to go into a building full of dusty old tomes, legends, and myths, he honestly didn't know.

She's a strange one, though, Xera. Not that she hasn't always been, and I am learning her habits through these many years, habits that drive me insane. I have been alive for eons and I am reduced to a naïve little girl's babysitter, someone who isn't even half my age yet. I deserve more; I need more. There is nothing to this task, no meaning, no drive. Nothing but a long hunt of the same thing and beings over thousands of years. Though I will admit, it is interesting to get to know my mark this time rather than just trying to make them die.

He stomped his foot and shook his head, forcing his mind to focus on the task at hand. How to get Xera to trust him. She clearly didn't yet, and he had made it worse this evening. She had no memories, but still, she was wary of him. Something that had enraged his mate. He reached up to touch the scratches on his face, too lazy to heal them. He sucked in a breath at the smarting pain that lanced along his cheek. For such a tiny woman, his mate truly packed power in her compact little body.

Duff shuddered and shifted. There had been something different in the air this evening. An impatience, desperation. He had seen it gleaming in the Guardian's eyes. Had seen the obsession of his lover already beginning to glare out at the world.

"He is getting desperate, and there is nothing more dangerous than a desperate man, especially when his love is the reason for the desperation. He is falling for her sooner this time, quicker than all the others times. And he is starting to notice things quicker this time."

Duff shifted and shook his head. Too much heavy thinking and without a backward glance, he slid his hand across the scratches in his face, making them disappear and then walked out the door, his glamor back in place. It was time to prowl. Maybe he could find a sweet little honey just to vent some frustration on. Surely his mate wouldn't mind that; as long as he wasn't carnal, Tamesis would be alright. He'd save that for her when he got home, but she better be ready, because he would be ravenous.

Duff strolled along the small streets, a permanent smile etched on his face, and he hated every minute of it. Hands in his denim jeans, he strutted and whistled softly to himself, knowing that the glamor he had chosen for this night was perfect. It was a Friday night and some college broad somewhere would be too drunk to stand, and he would find her, he always did. Then when they found her in the morning, broken and battered, beaten and dead, it would mean his night was worth it.

He growled quietly to himself, shaking his head at the clamoring of the street noises. They pressed against his sensitive ears, causing a thumping to begin in their middles and pushing into his temples. The swish of tires and the splash of rainwater as the tires rolled through the puddles. The sound of the street vendors calling to the night owls that walked out and around. The people that leaned from their windows and doorways to holler at each other or hurl insults at the couples that strolled by.

Duff felt the burn of vitriol at the back of his throat at the high, girlish giggles of the woman in the local bars and the men as they whispered their special lines in their ears, anxious to get them home.

These disgusting humans, the playthings of the gods, and us demons alike, they have no qualms. They are mindless, disgusting, thoughtless pieces of bones and meat wrapped in skin. Easily broken, yet their spirits, so willing, so full, so unlike those of the nether and the heavens. It's a shame that they will all die at my mother and Tamesis's hands. Though I do like to break them myself. It is a beautiful sound, the breaking of bones and the crying; It is fulfilling.

A smile slid along his jaw, razor sharp and full of charm. His smile was squelched as a car drove by and splashed him with rain water. He waved his hand and watched in the nearby shop window in delight as the car flipped and flew and just like that, a few more souls to add to his mother's garrison. A chuckle worked its way out of his mouth, dark and menacing. As darkness continued to lay its heavy head down over the land and even more of his brethren joined him in the streets, his eye caught the perfect little number for his night time play.

He stared at her blonde hair as bright as a sunflower and the wide blue eyes in her head, darkened with smears of dark mascara and tinted blue shadow. She held a simpering gaze, and it was clear that she had taken into her gullet way too much alcohol. However, that made it all the more perfect. Duff strolled up to her as she stared about in confusion and smiled.

"Hello there, Sweetheart. You look like you need a helping hand. I'm Dwayne. Can I help you get home?"

She nodded, and his smile grew, though his eyes glittered darkly.

I am looking forward to this.

He held out his arm. "Shall we? Which way did you say home was? A beautiful young woman like you shouldn't be out here alone."

CHAPTER 13

RYDER

Ryder stared at the picture on the front page of the paper, his horror growing with each word he read. Finally, he leaned back in his chair and covered his eyes. It was happening all over again, the horrifying happenings of his birthday. A woman found murdered in her own home, torn apart and broken. The only reason the police were even able to tell who she was were her teeth. He rubbed his eyes and then his chest, a pain burrowing deep into his heart.

Perhaps I shouldn't have come home? Does that man, no, that creature because no man would be that evil. Does he know I am back? Is this why it's happening again? Perhaps it is a blessing to have my memories torn asunder; perhaps I am not meant to remember such horrors.

Ryder brushed at his temples, digging his fingers into them, anxiety rippling along his back, as his memories surged from the onslaught of violent photographs in front of him. A man in his past, a man who had turned his arm into a bowl of jelly with one placed hit from a baseball bat. Ryder clutched his arm and shook his head, fighting to dispel such grisly thoughts. Violence was a terrible thing, something he had and always would hate. Though he wasn't afraid to take care of himself if needed.

A double standard if I ever heard of one, but why let someone beat you up? Why let someone hurt you that way? There is no reason to be that vulnerable; that is one lesson I learned well. I don't even need my memories to know that is the truth.

Ryder pushed the paper aside with shaking fingers and stared unseeing at the top of his wooden desk. He pulled a piece of paper forward and began to sketch a picture of the wings that he had been seeing in his head over and over in all his dreams. Making sure to take the time to line each feather, gently and kindly. As he scribbled, his mind wandered to the matter at hand, the women being hurt, three in the last couple of weeks, the memories that he wanted to find but also couldn't even after weeks of perusing the periodicals and the archives, looking for something, anything to connect the dots of his past and form a picture.

Perhaps all this violence is just the idiots gearing up for Halloween. Everyone knows that's when the violent and the angry come out. One day a year that they can show their true colors, and some, some of them go too far.

Ryder shuddered, hating Halloween, he always had. He shook his head.

There's just something terribly wrong with a Holiday where you can hide your true face. And far too many people use it to prey on the innocent and the naïve, those like Xeraphina. Xera, I wonder where she is? It's been some time since I've seen her in the library, and it was clear that she likes to read. Perhaps that idiot that follows her around like a puppy dog keeps her away. He clearly needs some books in his life, though. He's an imbecile. I hope above all else he keeps her safe. There's a madman on the loose.

Ryder stared moodily down at the drawing in front of him, the colors a strange contrast with each other, the black with the white band. He turned his gaze to the window and felt Xera's absence like a small pain. It was strange for him to miss someone he barely knew. If there was one thing that could be said of Ryder Greer, he never missed anyone. A lesson he had learned the quickest of all while in the foster care system for what he felt was the worst year of his life. You didn't make friends; they usually left quicker than it took to gain their trust. It was a discipline he had continued on with well into his adult years. Except for his cats, Ryder had no ties.

Our brief encounters, though, they are nice, and it shows that I have been lacking in certain areas of my life. Foolish, really, of me, to get attached after only a few surprising meetings, but there is just something. Perhaps she just reminds me too much of some wounded creature. From now on, I need to just forget about her, not worry about where she is or what she is doing. Clearly, our conversations aren't as meaningful as I think they are to her.

Ryder began to clean up his desk and the area surrounding it, anxious now for his day to just be over. He was in dire need of a coffee and his animals happy distraction. He was startled from his thoughts by the large oak door opening, and he came face to face with the woman he had just been thinking of. An unconscious smile graced his face, which she returned the same shyly.

His brown eyes met her blue ones, and he stood still for a moment, drinking in their deep blue color. He shifted and shrugged sheepishly and filled the now deafening silence.

"Hello, Miss McCall. How may I help you today?"

He backed further up, putting more distance between himself and her, anxiety rippling across his shoulders. His face darkened as he fought to keep calm, something he hated. He was naturally a calm person. He had been forced to be.

But this woman, this tiny little woman, she changes things and I don't know why. I've worked too long and too hard for all these years to make sure that the world outside and the people in it don't affect me. But she with her innocence and that naïve little face of hers. She just makes everything feel all vulnerable and raw. It's not fair.

He blinked in surprise when he realized she too had shifted and was staring at him a little bit strangely, and he realized she must have spoken.

"I'm sorry, can you repeat that?"

Xera smiled and dipped her head, tugging at her side-swept hair. "I asked if you did that drawing there on your desk? It's beautiful."

Ryder looked down and shrugged, lifting the picture in his hands and holding it out. "Yes, it's nothing really, just some scribbles to kill some time."

Xera tugged it from his hands and stared at it. She ran feather-light fingertips across it and smiled gently. "Well, for scribbles, it's gorgeous. You have such talent, it looks so lifelike. The details are so crisp. Where did the idea come from?"

She looked up and met his gaze, a quizzical expression on her face. Ryder mentally groaned and shook his head. Tasting the bitter lie on his tongue. "Just drew it. Didn't really think about where it came from."

Xera gave him a small nod and held it out to him. "Well, it's beautiful. You should enter it into the art contest they have. I saw it on the school activities board. Well, unless staff can't?"

She frowned in thought. "Sorry, I didn't really think about that. But really, you should see if you can."

Ryder chuckled quietly and laid it back down to his desk. "No thank you. I just drew it to pass some time. I prefer not to have attention. Anyway, can I help you with something today?"

"Oh yes. I need some help finding some books. Mr. Hennessey gave us a research project to work on, and I'm afraid I am at a loss of what to look for."

Xera gazed up at him, and Ryder stiffened as his breathing grew tight, and he was certain he could hear his heart in his ears. He hung on her every word, the simple question she asked in the innocent voice of hers, soft and sweet; it was pleasing to his ears. Chills skittered up his spine and sweat pooled beneath his arms. He sucked in a tight breath at the astronomical feelings she invoked upon him. He forced his breath through his teeth on a whistle. It was foolish to act this ridiculous over a young woman that he had spoken to barely a handful of times.

"And please call me Xera. I really don't like Miss McCall. It makes me sound like an old maid." The smile she offered him was mischievous and kind.

Ryder dipped his head. "Alright, Xera. What is your paper on? I can find some resources for you better that way."

Xera laughed and touched her head. "Oh yes, I'm sorry." She pulled a slip of paper from the baby blue bag that adorned her shoulders. "I am to write how religious legends are turned into myths. I thought maybe it would be interesting to write about fallen angels and lead from there. I really want to make this paper great, so any help I would really appreciate."

She returned her gaze to him, holding out the paper. There was hope in her eyes, and it made his heart fall to his knees. He gave a soft cough and looked around to make sure no one else needed him before he settled into helping her with her project.

Ryder turned and motioned for her to follow him. "Well, for starters, let's see what I can find for you. I can also tell you a bit of what I know if you like? I am by no means a genius on the subject, but a little bit."

She met his gaze and nodded. "Oh please, do tell."

Ryder held up his hand and continued speaking, turning once to check that she was following him. "Firstly, it really depends on who you talk to and which religion you want to base it on. Because there is knowledge in almost all the religions that could lead you then into your myths from there. For instance, some people believe that the only fallen angels are those that fell when Satan fell. Others believe they are those that turned their backs on their leader, their god, whether it was for revenge or love or lust, but something to make them face the dark side of life. There is also the whole fight or contention between the believers that these fallen angels can be redeemed in some way."

Xera listened with rapt attention, and Ryder blushed when she smiled and spoke. "What a great start for me to look. Thank you so much, Ryder. I take it you like to learn a lot of new things? Being a librarian and all?"

Ryder chuckled and held out a seat for her and answered her while he pulled some books from the shelves. "Well, you could say that. I do love to learn new things. I have a few degrees as well. I figure, why stop at one thing when you can learn so much? And there's so much knowledge out there, it is amazing really."

The door to the front of the library opened. The sound was loud in the quiet building, and Ryder turned to look balling his fists at his sides. He gritted his teeth. He hated people abusing the building he was responsible for. He cursed under his breath when his brown eyes met the hazel eyes of the idiot that followed Xera around.

"Your friend is here."

Xera looked up from the books she was

perusing and smiled and waved. "Oh yes, I asked him to come. We have the same class. I don't know what his paper's on, though. Maybe you can help him too?"

Ryder fought to keep his irritation in check. He didn't want to help him. He crossed his arms, and he knew he was pouting in a way, but he really didn't care.

Why would she bring him here? She knows very well we can't stand each other, especially after that last horrific meeting. What is wrong with me? Why does it even matter if they are friends? Listen to me, being foolish over a woman that I don't even know that well.

Ryder forced himself to calm down and nodded his head and spoke through tight lips. "Gladly, if he needs it."

Ryder balked as the man met his gaze and the smirk danced along his face. Ryder wanted to punch it right off his jaw. Instead, he gave a tight-lipped smile and spoke through gritted teeth. "Hello, Duff, right? I was helping Xera here with finding some books. Do you need some help as well?"

Duff settled across from her and looked up at Ryder, another smug expression on his face as he lounged backward. "Nah, I know my way around, thanks. I was here last year."

Xera looked up and chuckled. "Oh, yea. This is my first year and Duff's second."

Duff looked to Ryder again and spoke. "I think we're good; we'll call if we need you." Ryder shifted and, glaring, stomped away.

How dare he talk to me like I am some sort of servant? Like some animal to be forced into his bidding. And Xera didn't even notice. How awful is that? Why am I worried about it anyway? Stupid, Ryder, stupid. Getting attached. You know this never ends well. Why does she even put up with him like that? Ridiculous.

Ryder settled into his own chair and, growling, threw his picture in the trash. He rubbed his temples, anxious and irritable. He stared at the paper with the poor girl on the front blown up and bold for everyone to see. Everyone to see her pain, and he growled and pushed it away.

Perhaps that is just my problem. My mother was like, what I can remember. Naïve of the workings of people. One of the reasons I probably have this scar on my face and all the others on my body. Too fearful to speak up clearly; there's no other reason for it. She had to be naïve like Xeraphina. Perhaps that is why I am so drawn to her, someone like my mother, a way to find memories or form new ones. Who knows?

Ryder tugged at the ends of his hair, the ache easing from his temples. The rest of the day was uneventful, if annoying having to watch Xera and Duff talking together. Ryder shooed the last of the stragglers from the building and locked the door. He was more than ready to go home.

Ryder turned on the news, his first mistake of the evening, clear after the vegetable soup he had just made roiled and bubbled throughout his guts. He stared at the woman on the news channel, her mouth moving, but all he heard was silence, the buzzing in his ears far too loud. What had that young woman been thinking on her last night on earth? Surely it hadn't been what she had to go through. She had probably expected to go home that night and get some rest.

Ryder slammed his hand across his mouth, the burn of bile deep in his throat, and he ran toward his bathroom. He barely made it before he watched as the vegetables and chunks of meat swirled around in the scummy water. The water made him dizzy, and he closed his eyes tight.

Behind the darkness of his lids, he saw in his mind's eye, a puddle of blood on a dark floor and feathers plastered all around. He groaned as he opened his eyes again, slamming himself back to the present time and again vomit rose up in his throat. He stared at the cold tile floor, unsure how his cheek had come to rest on the mosaic of black and white. He groaned and sat up, brushing at his eyes and the pain behind them. His fingers came away with wet tips and a salty freshness coated his lips. He stared at his fingers with a slack jaw and wiped them on his shirt as quick as he could.

"What is happening!"

He screamed at the ceiling, unsure what was going on and why he was so angry. All day over nothing he had been angry. It started with a news story, moved to a slip of a girl, and back to a news story. It wasn't fair, and the memories that he had long forgotten were resurfacing all day, and now his thoughts raced and the pictures that danced behind his eyelids and in his mind's eye were awful. And they made no sense.

What is going on? Why is all this happening? I wanted to know, I wanted the memories, but not like this, not this fast, and the violence. There is so much violence in my life. It is no wonder that I had forgotten it. Terrible things keep stirring up. What should I do? It hurts to even move; the thoughts are like barbs to my brain. ARGH.

He walked on shaky legs toward his bedroom, pulling at his clothes and turning off the lights, anxious for his silk sheets and a hopefully dreamless sleep.

Ryder was on a mission. He was looking for

someone, a young woman. It was demanded of him, his duty to find her and guard her. It was his job. There was an added urgency to his step as he forced himself through the woods, the long dirt path, brambles tugged and nipped at his heels, but he continued. A clearing came into view, and his heart clenched deep within his chest. He shook his head. There was a sense of admiration now, of happiness, and it all centered on the small woman that stood in the clearing. He sighed in relief and hurried toward her, not noticing that her face was obscured with a blur of strangeness.

The long, blue dress that she wore touched the very edge of her shoes, obsidian toes peeping out from underneath. A bonnet of startling white sat atop her long, brown hair, making her hair darker and the blue eyes that peered at him glimmer with a shade of color he did not recognize.

Anticipation skittered down his spine, and the hairs along his arm and neck rose as he leaned forward, a sense of urgency forcing him to move even quicker toward her. He needed to get her from the clearing and now. There was something wrong, very wrong. There was a darkness there at the edges of the clearing, a tickle of fear digging at his soul. There was something about the girl, something that resonated.

He shifted his weight as he got near her and gazed around in surprise as the area around him melted to form another time, a different place. She was there, holding his hand, the pad of her thumb rubbing along the ridge of his wrist in comforting circles.

"I know you don't like crowds, but thank you so much for bringing me here. Especially on All Hallow's Eve."

Her voice echoed and rebounded around him as if it were down a tunnel long away. He looked around, taking in the festival around them, women and men and children running and dancing, feasting on bright red apples, masks obscuring their faces. He turned to take in her gaze, fighting to see anything past the blurred veil that concealed her face.

He turned to meet the other gazes of the partygoers, to match the disappointment they showered him with, to glare and lift his head just a little bit higher. There was an unspoken feeling of the rules being broken, that he had done it, but he didn't care, couldn't care. She belonged to him.

He pulled her closer, staring in distaste at the shadows along the walls, the way they seemed to take on a life of their own. She whispered to him, her voice stirring his blood.

"Are you okay, my love? There are no demons here. Just the guardians and those they protect, you know this. They are not allowed here. Besides, if they do come, you will protect me."

Ryder looked around, rubbing his glove-clad hand along his thigh. "They are allowed here, it is a place of neutrality, they just do not come here. There are no souls for them to take. And we guardians, there are less and less of us left. There are not mortals blessed to care for. I am the last of my kind."

He squeezed her hand, grazing his own thumb across her knuckles, letting her know he understood and he was there. He stiffened as a deep heat blew from the side of the area, his own core heating up as the smell of dead leaves and sulfur stirred his nose. He searched frantically on all sides, searching for the leather-clad woman he knew belonged to such lustful intoxication. He froze in abject horror as he saw fear in the faces of the mortals and the guardians. There was violence on the air, and the metallic scent of blood mixed with the sweet smells of the festival.

The shadows expanded and swallowed the mortals and their guardians, and the screams reverberated through the air. Ryder pulled his love closer, and he grabbed the knife at his waist as a woman materialized from the nearest shadows.

Eyes of deep black peered at him from a face of pure white. The red of her lips made Ryder think of juicy apples and raspberries. He licked his lips, taken back by her beauty but also the evil that emanated from her core. Her clothes left nothing to the imagination as she sidled closer and despite the fear and the anger, he felt momentary longing.

"Lilith, you know this is a place of neutrality."

The woman simpered up at him, her long lashes hiding the emptiness of her gaze. "Oh, silly me, was it not that earth was neutral ground until your mother took what was mine? So, I shall take what is hers."

Ryder spat at her feet. "You are nothing more than Cain's lover. You are nothing. You can take nothing."

The woman cursed, and then Ryder felt falling and a voice reverberated on all sides, causing him to push his hands hard against his ears.

"I love him. He is mine. Your father. No."

Ryder woke with a loud gasp and clutched at his chest, trying to force air through his lungs, but to no avail. He was fighting to live in the throes of a panic attack. A small, furry face rubbed against his own. The purring of his pal's voice resonated throughout him, and he took one long breath and then another. He moaned aloud as every part of his body burned and ached, and then it slowly began to ebb. The resulting residue of a dream gone terribly wrong.

He stood on shaky limbs, digging his feet into the plush carpet.

This is real. This is home. It was nothing more than a nightmare, nothing more than a dream. These dreams are going to kill me soon, though, if I don't figure it out. Crazy innuendos, faceless women and things that are not human.

CHAPTER 14

XERA

Xera sat in the lunchroom staring out into the gray day. So many of those in October. She frowned in disgust and rubbed her knee. So much pain when the day was cold and wet. Xera wasn't sure if she would ever have no pain, but she doubted it at this point, and that was disappointing. The young woman sighed and looked back out into beyond.

She kept catching her gaze on the tall bell tower of the library, the only piece of the old building she could see. She was loath to admit it was more than the library that held her attention and called to her. The man who took care of it, she found him fascinating. Ryder Greer, what a lovely name he had. Strong and fitting for such a fellow.

Xera blushed and touched her cool hands to her warm cheeks.

If I'm honest, he scares me. Well, not him exactly, but my reaction to him. It's silly to be this enamored with someone I barely know. It's almost like a moth to a flame, these feelings, wants.

She was startled out of her thoughts by a loud thump as Duff sat down, his plate clanging to the tabletop.

"Thinking about that librarian again, are you? Strange man, he is."

He bit into his burger with a growl. Xera wrinkled her nose, pulling her plate closer to her own space.

"Duff. You don't know that. You don't know what's in my head or what I am thinking. I am not thinking of him."

Xera licked her lip and sighed distastefully at the small white lie.

Duff snorted and stared at her, humor on his face. "Of course I do. It's written all over your face. Also, you cannot lie; you are terrible at it. And you are still wearing the sweatshirt he gave you from like two weeks ago. I'm not stupid, Xera. You are obsessed with him. What would your mom say? About you already forming an attraction to someone like that. You know nothing about him. He could be crazy or abusive."

Xera hugged her arms tightly around her body, upset at his sparing use of her mother's thoughts.

Mother wouldn't care, would she? No, of course she wouldn't. I am not obsessed, I just find him attractive. There's nothing wrong with that, even Duff knows that, and Mom would have said the same thing. Nothing wrong with that.

Xera squared her shoulders. "I am an adult, Duff. I am twenty-four years old, and were my mother still alive, she would say nothing of the kind. And you know nothing about him, and trust me, he is not abusive. There is nothing that points to such a thing."

Duff shifted and bit into a fry. "Perhaps you're right. But how can you really know?"

He held up a fry and pointed it at her. "Mark my words, though. Those intellectual types like that, they can't form bonds of any kind. They can't please a woman, not like us normal people can. They are all smarts and no physical prowess. No game."

It was Xera's turn to snort. Duff shrugged. "It's true."

Xera lifted her plate and raised a brow. "Whatever you say, Duff. But I happen to think there are more important things than physical prowess, as you so put it."

Xera pulled the green sweatshirt tighter around

her shoulders as she stood. "Regardless, and as enlightening as this conversation is, I do need to go to the library. This report won't write itself. You coming?"

Duff shook his head, glaring at the fry in his hand. "Naw, I have a tutoring session." He scowled even deeper. "She's not even hot."

Xera laughed, waved, and walked away, anxious to get away from Duff and his strange conversation.

Xera stood staring up at the tall doors, Duff's words in her head about her clear infatuation. She sighed. He had just reiterated the thoughts she had already been thinking herself, which made it all the harder to swallow. Xera shook her head and leaned forward to push the large doors open. She was caught off guard by the number of students in the library. She nibbled at her lip. She should have known there would be more; the deadline for their reports was getting closer. Ryder was helping a small group of giggling girls, and she felt a small tendril of jealousy nip at her back, but she tightened her hands into her straps and took the moment to drink him in. The blue shirt that he wore made his tan skin all the more enticing. And the dark, intense expression of thought on his face was alluring. She smiled and then turned to find a spot to spread her own books and reports out.

Ryder walked up to her, hands in his faded jean pockets and a small smile on his face.

"The sweatshirt looks good on you."

Xera looked down, and her cheeks flamed. "Oh, I'm sorry. I should have given it back. Honestly, I –"

Ryder held up his hand, chuckling. "It's okay. It was getting too small for me, and its fate was for the cat's bed, so I am glad it is getting some good use. And besides, it looks great on you. As I said."

Xera shifted and looked at the table again. "Thanks."

Ryder leaned back on the heels of his feet. "You here for the same reason all of them are? Last minute writing of the report for Mr. Hennessey? Or did you actually come to see me?"

Xera laughed as she moved her backpack toward the nearest table and laid it down. "Yes, and of course I came to see you. I am almost completely done, just a few more tweaks and some last minute tidbits of information and I'll be good. I'm pretty proud of it. I'll have to get you to read it sometime."

Ryder pulled out her chair, motioning for her to sit, and after she had sat, he sat across from her, folding his arms across his chest and leaning back into the chair, sighing blissfully.

"First time I've sat all day, and I'd like that. So, tell me about yourself, Xera, for a moment before you start working on your paper?"

Xera giggled and nodded. "Gladly, though there isn't much to tell. This is my first year of college. I wasn't ready to come when I was younger and then I was in an accident about a year or two ago and had some recovery to do before I could do anything else, and well, a loss to get over."

Xera looked down, a frown replacing her smile as she thought of her mother and how much she was missing. There was so much she wished to share with her.

She was startled as a big hand covered her own small one and squeezed. "I am sorry, Xera. That does not seem very fair and losses are hard to get over. Trust me, I know that."

Xera sniffled but smiled and squeezed his hand back. Ryder shifted and spoke. "You have healed well, though, I hope"

Xera nodded. "For the most part. I still hurt when the weather is disgusting like today. But it is just a normal part of life now. Tea helps and sometimes pain pills, but they are gross. So I only take them if I have too."

They both turned as the door was pushed open and another group of students popped in. "Excuse me, Xera. I hope we can continue this conversation again sometime."

Xera's cheeks warmed again as he walked by, touched her shoulder and squeezed. She held her hand to the spot after he left, holding onto the little bit of warmth that was still leeched in. It was nice to have someone to talk too just about everyday life. Someone who didn't make life vulgar or disgusting.

Xera smiled to herself and busied herself with her report. Only a few more paragraphs and she would be able to type it and turn it in.

Xera limped toward her apartment, her cheeks burning as the wind licked them with fiery fingers. She brushed at her stinging eyes, anxious to get home and out of the cold. As she unlocked her door and stepped inside, the silence greeted her. She sighed softly and looked around, regretting not having someone or something to say hello when she arrived Today, the silence was lonely. Xera lay her books on the nearby coffee table and made a beeline for the bath; a warm bath always helped her pain. Xera lay lazily in the tub, her one hand dangling over the side. Her thoughts raced, and she dwelled on the feelings Ryder invoked in her. The raw, vulnerable feelings she hadn't touched in some time.

What should I do about this? These feelings are literally plaguing my every waking thought and dream. It is not a terrible thing, but I need to make a decision soon. It seems so forward to mention to him. But I also don't want to just ignore it. There could be greatness here. Ugh.

Xera continued to relax in the tub, her mind returning to Ryder. Closing her eyes, she was seized by a momentary feeling of fear. Her heart clenched and her throat closed and she couldn't breathe. She screamed and slapped the water as she felt hands rise up from below and wrap around her shoulders, dragging her down. Down into the dark, murky depths of the deep water. She screamed soundlessly, bubbles erupting from her mouth. She needed to get out of the water right now as voices whispered all around her.

"I killed you before, I can do it again."

The water was dark and blurry; nothing could be seen.

Xera lurched out of the tub with a scream. She heaved over the side and stared at the pristine walls and bright lights. No darkness, no people, just her bathroom. She pushed herself from the tub and ran, banging her leg as she did so. Xera sat on her bed, a blanket wrapped tightly around her shoulders as she rocked back and forth. It was going to be a long night. She curled to her side, anxious to try and ease the ache and the sadness and the fear with some sleep, dreamless sleep.

Hours later, Xera awoke screaming, tears pouring down her face and coating her tongue with saltiness. She struggled to sit up, tangling with her blankets and whimpering under her breath until she was able to reach her bedside lamp and turn it on. She sat heaving, running her fingers over her chest and arms, looking for the wounds that had been inflicted in the dream. She found none and shivered, wrapping her arms around her body.

There was so much blood and all the dark water and the pain. So much pain it felt like fire, everywhere, stabbing and bleeding. And feathers, black feathers. What is the deal with the feathers all over the ground? Why! Why am I having such terrible nightmares? They're getting worse. They haven't been this bad since I was a child.

Xera fought to stem the flow of her tears while forcing herself to take deep breaths, calming the heaving in her chest. She stared at her fingers, rubbing them up and down again on her blanket, certain that the feeling of sticky wetness of blood still clung to them. She shuddered and rubbed her eyes, trying to get rid of the offending aftermath of her nightmares.

I really need my mom.

Xera held her hands to her chest, wishing with all her might her mother was still alive. "I would even settle for some of her tea."

Xera sniffled and gave a small smile at the memory of her mother and the special tea she made. She should have asked her where she got it; she should have asked her mother so much more. Xera stifled another sob and shook her head.

Xera shifted and spoke to the silence. "I need more friends. More friends than just Duff or Ryder, as wonderful as they both may be. I don't imagine either one would appreciate a sobbing woman showing up on their doorstep. I should make more effort to meet other people."

Xera leaned back into her pillows, frowning as she reached for the pile of books on her side table.

"Might as well do something productive with my time now that I'm wide awake."

CHAPTER 15

DUFF

Duff sat staring at the wall with hooded eyes, holding a stiff drink in his hand. He spoke to the silence through gritted teeth.

"I hate him. No, I loathe him. So many wasted lifetimes chasing him and his bride. Repeating our failures over and over, I can't fail this time. Tamesis needs this, but why does she need this one? More like my mother needs this and, as always, there's a pawn. This time it is Tamesis. Though if we prevail, well, all the better for both women. But if we fail, we lose our leverage to get the older Greer."

He screamed and threw his glass at the wall, snarling as it shattered into a million pieces. He sighed and leaned back into his chair, rubbing his eyes and cursing while his mind went in racing circles.

I am failing again. Never have we truly beat him, and now, again, we are failing. Xera does not trust me as she does Ryder, even with no memories. The ancient binding of the two is too strong. This plan must work to keep my Tamesis forever. I don't understand why, after all these years, we changed the plan. Before, we just killed them both and were done with it. Why can't their deaths just give Tamesis what she wants? Why must there be a ritual?

Duff slammed his hand on the oak table near him. "So many other ways to gain immortality. Why must she have this one and right now of all times? You never trust a Seer. I've told her so many times." He snorted and rolled his eyes. "Especially not my mother's Seer. Their memories are coming fast this time, but still, they dance around them, afraid. Perhaps if I can find a way to keep their memories at bay, make them seem crazy"

Duff tapped his fingers restlessly.

This ritual only happens once every so many years, so Tamesis and I must be ready. We cannot fail, not this time. It would spell disaster for her, for me, for Mother. The one thousandth day of the one thousandth year is coming fast upon us. I need to figure this out, figure out how to give Tamesis and my mother both what they want.

Duff shook his head and squeezed his fingers together, fisting them open and shut. "Mortals and their counting, three hundred and sixty-five days a year, ridiculous. So short sighted. No realization that their days are much shorter than reality. Always walking around with their eyes closed. Fools."

He sighed and stared out the darkened window. "It's no wonder they have learned nothing, no secrets of the outer realms, not even their own mistakes. If we are to walk among them again, it must be kept that way."

He ran a hand across his haggard face. He looked around and scowled as he thought of the seer again.

This is all her fault. If she hadn't whispered into Tamesis's ear, told her that stupid prophecy, I would not be here, and they would both already be dead. What is that stupid thing anyway? Oh yes. On the darkest night of the darkest day, an evil will come forth of ancient breath. The innocent will stand with the fallen, and the light will shine below. It is with black dagger the fire of the fallen shall fall by evil's chosen hand. Innocence shall land, and the immortal chain will be forged. Whether it is by fallen or evil has yet to demand. So I get the darkest night and day, that is the thousandth day. And Tamesis is the evil from ancient breath. Of course the innocent is Xera, and she will stand with her lover, the fallen. But what does it mean the chain? Is there a chance it will all backfire?

Duff snorted as he reached for another drink. "Naught but nonsense and riddles."

At the soft patter of feet, he turned to meet the angry blue eyes of his mate, her body vibrating in fury. She paced in front of him, the short skirt she wore riding up each time she moved. He smirked as he watched her, taking note of each line and curve. All his.

"We only have weeks. And you sit here nursing a drink and making a mess of the place. The plan, Duff, why aren't you following the plan!"

Duff shrugged. "It's not working. Her bond is too strong. I can't make her trust me. I told you this was futile. That there were other ways. But no, you and Mother need this to work. Ridiculous. We will need to follow mother's plan now."

"What! Then kill him. I don't need him, just his precious princess. His memories will be back soon, you idiot. You are a chaos demon, so start acting like it."

She crossed her arms, her chest heaving. He took a moment to leer before grabbing her arm until she whimpered and dragging her forward. He bent forward and whispered in her ear.

"Idiot! How dare you call me such names. I have killed others for less. Just because you are my mate does not mean I won't strike you next time. I have told you, sweetheart, it is not that simple. And mother told you we could not harm the Greer. Are you really so ambitious that you don't think my mother wouldn't let that disobedience lie?"

He backed up and twisted her arm so she continued to look at him, a pained expression on her face. "I know very well his memories are there, but I can do nothing to him until your precious ritual day. His mother is the Seer of the angels and his father a Greer and the most powerful guardian to ever walk among the ancient ones. Ryder's powers are astronomical, so I cannot kill him on my own anyway. Nor will I. I will not face my mother's wrath, Tam. Do you realize Greers were made to slaughter my kind? That is why they were breathed into existence to be able to battle against those that are of darkness and win?"

Duff shoved her away and downed the rest of the bottle. He slammed it on the table with a smack of his lips and stared at her as she jumped.

"He is also guarded by one of the first guardians, and the library is neutral ground. I can do nothing there. We are in the middle of a war zone, Tam. Two cosmic beings at war, so our plans matter little. You think those are the only plans in play. You don't think my mother wants retribution for Trinity Greer stealing the soul of Kavi? The only guardian to ever be swayed by lust's own whispers, but his soul swayed back by a seer. We are small compared to them, Tam, and if we do not follow our role to the letter, there will be nothing left of us. Especially if my mother gets a hold of us. So just shut up and play your role."

Tamesis stared at him wide-eyed, she growled once, but she nodded and sidled closer, licking her ruby red lips. "Need a massage, my love?"

Duff's body slackened, and he nodded, smirking at her and raising a suggestive eyebrow.

Chapter 16

Ryder

Ryder lounged on the bench, the collar of his coat turned up against the biting wind. He took a deep breath. At the moment, his mind was peaceful. More than he could say for the days and nights prior. The nights plagued with nightmares and the days with bad memories. Ryder shifted, blinking his eyes. He bit the inside of his jaw, thinking of the dreams and memories.

Perhaps I should start worrying about my sanity. Maybe I'm pushing for answers too hard and all the attacks on the women aren't helping, just like when I was a teen. This was how it started then, and now it's back again. All these dreams of blood and monsters and voices calling. It makes no sense. I just... Maybe I need a break. But how can I take one? I am needed, and I can't just give up searching. I could possibly find an answer that the police haven't found if I dig deep enough in my memories and find something.

Ryder ran a hand through his hair and checked the watch around his wrist. He scowled as the date of November 11th flashed across the face of the watch.

Mom's birthday, surprising that I can remember that I suppose; not much else is there to hold onto. Add it to the very few things I can remember of her. Her free-falling hair that always went everywhere. Usually in my food.

Ryder chuckled as he remembered how she always used to know he was going to do something she disagreed with. She called it her mother magic, and usually, she could talk him out of it too. Ryder rubbed his eyes, fighting the burning and the itching. He shook his head, trying to focus on something other than his mother and how much he missed her.

He looked around, wondering what Xera was up to on such a cold day. They had spoken on and off, but she was very busy with her college work. She had finished her essay for her religion class. He smiled as he remembered Mr. Hennessey telling him it was one of the best he had seen in some time. Ryder grinned at the pride that swelled in his breast for her. He yawned as a burst of sleepiness hit him in the face.

He closed his eyes and leaned back against the bench, face tilted toward the little bit of sunlight to be had. He tightened his jacket around him and sighed.

I am exhausted, sleep a distant memory. These nightmares are horrendous. The only good things are stolen moments of conversation with Xera and my cats. I don't even feel human anymore.

Ryder wrinkled his nose as he felt eyes on him, caressing him like that of a lover. They lingered on his face, and he shifted and crossed his arms, loathe to open his eyes. Especially when he was finally comfortable. In his relaxing state, there were no memories, no nightmares more of the positive to not opening his eyes. He was drawn from his thoughts by a sweet voice calling to him.

"Hello, Ryder."

Ryder's eyes opened quickly, and he spied Xera. He leaned forward, a smile on his face as he drank her in.

"How are you doing today?" At her question, she kept blue eyes trained on his face. His chest tightened as he kept her gaze. He patted the seat beside him and leaned back again.

"Hey, Xera. Come sit with me? And you know, I'm not sure how I really am today. But I am glad to see you."

Xera settled beside him, tugging on the green

pea coat she wore. She tilted her head to look at him and gave a slow smile.

"What do you mean you don't know how you are? It's a beautiful day. I like to think I am pleasant company most of the time. So why such the long face?"

Ryder shrugged and folded his hands. He lifted one side of his lips in a strange, wary smile. "It's just been a bad couple of weeks, I guess. You know how I am starting to remember more from my past right?"

Xera leaned forward and nodded her head. "Yes, we've briefly talked about it."

"Well, those memories aren't the best, and I really miss my mom. And today, well today is her, or I guess would be, her birthday were she still around. And I just find that it's not a good day, despite the beautiful yet chilly weather." Ryder gave a forced laugh at his attempt at being nice and witty.

Xera covered his hand gently and smiled. "I know how that is. I miss my mom daily. I am sorry you lost your mom so young, Ryder. Would you like to talk about her? That helps me sometimes."

Ryder shrugged his shoulders and spoke softly. "Not much to tell really. I lost her when I was 17. Her name was Trinity. I miss her. Well, you know, I guess it's more I miss what I think should have been. It's like she disappeared from my mind the same day she died. There's just nothing, just snapshots and scars. It's frustrating, to say the least."

Xera squeezed his hand, held his gaze with her own, and he continued. "I'm trying to remember more; it's one of the reasons I came back, took this job. But you know, the more I remember, the darker my thoughts. I have nightmares and dark thoughts, and the memories just seem to get uglier and uglier the more I remember, which in turn makes the dreams worse."

Ryder was thrown from the dark turn his thoughts were taking when Xera threw her arms around him and held him close. Ryder's sight swam as she hugged him, and her perfume pervaded his senses. Wildflowers, she smelled like wildflowers. His mouth was filled with a metallic taste, and he blinked, trying to clear the blurriness from his eyes. He growled when all he saw was blood and feathers. Tears licked down his cheeks as he rocked someone or something in his arms. Ryder gasped out loud when Xera touched his cheeks with her hands on either side.

"Ryder, Ryder are you okay?"

Ryder pushed away from her and stared around him, looking all around, his chest heaving. He ran his hands across his arms, his chest, trying to banish the feeling of sticky wetness that had clung to him.

Xera searched his face, making his heart drop even lower. "Are you okay? Why won't you answer me? What's wrong? I'm sorry if my hug upset you."

Ryder held up his hand and shook his head. "No, no it's okay, just give me a minute. Just..."

Xera curled inward as he stood and paced. He watched with regret as she looked down and away. He leaned forward and touched her shoulder until she looked back up at him.

"Xera, it is nothing that you did. Remember how I was just talking about bad thoughts?" Xera looked at him with red-stained cheeks and nodded her head.

Ryder gave her a shaky smile. "I'm sorry, really, it's nothing you've done. I just had a bad thought. I think I just haven't gotten enough sleep. Just one minute, please stay."

Ryder stared at her as she gave him a stiff nod and his sighed.

Stupid stupid Ryder. What is wrong with me? I wanted that hug, been wanting her touch since the day I met her if I am being honest. Then I go and act like an absolute fool and idiot, all of the above maybe. Why are bad dreams coming in the daytime? Is my mother's god punishing me for something? Did I do something to warrant some powerful beings displeasure, because it sure feels that way. What do I need to do to fix this? I just don't understand, but right now, I need to fix this mess with Xera.

His gaze found Xera's again, and he rubbed the back of his neck, anxious. He shifted and sat down next to her and grabbed her hand.

"Hey, Xera. I'm sorry about that. I think I just need some sleep. I haven't slept very well in a while. I promise I won't do anything like that again. So, how about to make it up to you we get some lunch tomorrow. My treat?"

Xera stared at him for a moment, her hand on her cheek as she studied him. "No more freak outs? You promise? Okay, then we'll get some lunch."

Ryder smiled and dipped his head. "Great. That's great. There's this little diner right around the corner from where I live. I can pick you up tomorrow. It's within walking distance."

Xera chuckled and shook her head. "No, it's okay. I'll meet you there. I like walks and that way I can see more of this charming area. It's so cute here."

Ryder smiled and nodded. "Alright, it's a date then, but can I walk you home?" He looked up at the darkening sky. "It's starting to get dark and with the recent events, I'd like that."

Xera looked at him and dipped her head, a blush staining her cheeks. "Okay, yes, you can walk me home. As long as you promise to tell me more about you. You're such a mystery man," she teased him gently.

Ryder chuckled and held out his arm. "If you must know, I will share. Shall we?"

Xera stood outside her front door, shifting from foot to foot while Ryder stood beside her. She kept taking quick glances up at him through her lashes, unsure how to take how he had acted earlier that day.

All I did was hug him and he shot up. I shocked him. I don't know what I did. What did I do wrong? He just freaked out and started pacing. I mean, maybe he was tired like he said he was. Maybe he really does need sleep, but nightmares and strange daydreams. Perhaps I just need to not worry about it. Even if the same things are sort of happening to me. After all, I've been having strange nightmares. Maybe it's this town. All of us are scared with that psycho running loose and killing girls. Yes, that just has to be it.

Xera finally looked up at him and smiled. "Thank you for walking me home, Ryder. I really appreciate it, and I am looking forward to seeing you tomorrow. I have some homework to do, so I'll be seeing you?"

Xera leaned up and motioned for him to lean down. She gave him a kiss on the cheek and, turning, pushed her door open and closed, pushing the lock into place with a click. She leaned her head against the door frame, touching her palms to hot cheeks and biting back a smile.

I am so glad I stopped today to see him, even if it wasn't as good as I thought it would be. I really wasn't going to stop and talk to him. I was just going to keep walking, but he looked so sad just sitting there all alone. And it was clear he's been not sleeping; his eyes had dark circles underneath them. I just couldn't leave him. He looked too handsome to walk away from. The dark hair that arched across his brow. Yeah, I wouldn't have been able to walk away even if I wanted too.

Xera shifted, moving about her tiny apartment. She repositioned things and pulled out what she would need to make tea. As she boiled the water for it, her mind went back to the man she had just walked home with.

How can one man have me so twisted up in knots? He's gorgeous, of course, and what a beautiful mind he has. He is so knowledgeable about so many subjects. It is truly amazing how he keeps so much up there. But that is it. He is damaged, and I fear maybe beyond repair, but I am drawn to him. He is a mystery, but a good man. I can feel it there underneath all that angst. And besides, I can't stay away from him even if I tried. There's just something about him that makes me want to be near him.

Xera was thrown from her thoughts by the tea kettle whistle, and she sighed as she pulled it from the stove, pouring it over top of her tea leaves. As she blew on the steam that curled out, she pulled her laptop from her desk and settled to the table top to do some research on the handsome man that had walked her home.

Maybe if I can find out the answers for him, maybe then he won't be so troubled. Maybe if he has the answers he can sleep. Be normal.

Xera smiled softly as she clicked through old news files, anxious to find out what had happened to the librarian.

CHAPTER 17

GIDEON

Gideon stood in the nearby alleyway watching as Ryder walked away from Xera's home on his way to his own. Gideon sighed and rubbed at his eyes wearily.

"Have they begun to dance around their emotions, start to show their promise and love again, old friend?"

Gideon turned to meet the dark eyes of his friend Kavi. "They are stubborn, very stubborn, but yes, they are relearning about each other. I seem to remember another couple just as stubborn, possibly more so."

Kavi chuckled and shrugged. However, he frowned and spoke in all seriousness after. "Really, though, is our plan working again? Will they be ready? Will we save them?"

Gideon sighed and nodded. "Yes, it is, and I think so. I hope so. But just as we are gathering our own forces, so is Lilith's forces growing. Lust always whispers to the unholy. I have to say, this new girl, this Tamesis, she worries me, Kavi. She is not supposed to exist, a soulless. It makes me shudder just thinking about it. She is not normal, not right. Nature did not design her."

Kavi shifted and nodded his head. He growled. "Yes, she is worrisome, but Xera will take care of her eventually. I have faith. Or Lilith will herself. We all know her temper, myself more than most."

Kavi coughed and spoke, his voice hoarse. "You are okay? I worry for your health. You should not have to be down here anymore."

Gideon sighed and shook his head. "I am tired, Kavi. I am weary of this fight and the deaths. I am tired of watching them die over and over again just to be reborn. I love them as if they were my own. But I will be glad when this is over and they finally win. And they can join us in the afterlife. I must see this mission through. Though I do admit, I grow weary of bloodshed. It is a wonder you haven't yet."

Kavi sighed and ran his hand through his hair, so much like his son. "I still have a lot to atone for. I still have a lot of redemption to win. I have hurt many people, angels, all sorts through the years."

Gideon looked at his old friend a frown on his face. "You and Ryder, so much alike. Always certain that you can do better, save more. Kavi, my dear friend, you cannot save them all, and it is not your job too. Though you do that job well. And you of all have been redeemed far more than you realize. I wish you did not bear your burdens so closely."

Kavi shifted and smiled sadly. "Perhaps someday I will have done enough to make up for my mistakes. Keep watching over him. Perhaps I deserve these burdens"

Gideon watched as Kavi backed into the shadows and disappeared, and he sighed again, rubbing his eyes. Gideon turned and walked slowly toward the library. He sighed and stopped to look up at the moon.

I am Gideon, the first Guardian of the mortals, and I can do nothing to help those I love, but guide. They are slowly realizing, but will it be enough this time? Will Xera save Ryder? Will it make Ryder whole and a Guardian again? There's so much against them, even their own kind. Hating them, binding them, forcing them to a life of wrath for crimes they didn't commit to begin with. And those they had, it was fate and her fickle sisters and no one can win against them. A battle of wills is coming between them and the soulless and her mate. They have to succeed, though. They will, they have; to there are no more chances left. They are certainly stubborn enough, especially that dear,

dear boy."

Gideon chuckled to himself as he thought of the youth he had guarded and trained. The youth who had been stubborn and born with a chip on his shoulder, put there by his father himself. He was a force to be reckoned with even as a child. He did not fear his father's scars, rather he stared bravely into his eyes.

I remember well the day that Ryder came to me to train and guard. It was both a wonderful day and a heartbreaking day when the orders came. For I knew the future for my young pupil. No other guardians would take him, such a charming boy, but so angry at the world, at the elders, at himself for being born. They said he was too stubborn, he was mixed blood, a blight on our lineage, there was a darkness in him. I ignored them all, anxious and pleased to take on the mentoring of my two friends' son. A young boy whom I love as my own. But was I enough, were his parents enough, is Xera enough? Can we fix him?

Gideon was thrown from his thoughts when a skittering sound assaulted the night. The alarm all Guardians knew and knew well. When they were tasked with protecting the innocents, the powerful mortals from the dark mother and her children. It meant a dark child was among them, and he or she was hunting. Gideon sniffed and searched the darkness for the innocent the demon was after. Stepping toward her when he located her but being forcefully stopped when her life force, her soul, waned and darkened. She now belonged to the shadows, a dark child to breed more. He sighed. How he hated that he had to let her go. He knew her, had seen her in the library. She was sweet with green eyes and long brown hair. However, he was not to break the balance, he was not to weaken the small tendril of control the elders still held, keeping their shaky truce in place. Though soon enough, that truce would end. They all knew it, but to end it early was certain death, or worse, banishment.

Gideon spoke in a whisper to the open air. "Oh, sweet mortals. So innocent and gracious, yet so easily corrupted by the dark world, by sweet murmurings in your ears of dark promises and sweet lies. I weep for you and always will."

Gideon turned and shuffled toward the library, now anxious to get home and sleep, to lay his head on his pillow and forget the day and its troubles. He was weary.

Chapter 18

Ryder

Ryder stepped into his foyer and let out a small growl as his cats batted his legs, digging their claws into his now bare feet. He lifted his feet, wincing as their tiny claws dug in and ripped the skin.

"I know, I know. I'm sorry. I'm late to feed you four. Forgive me? You all need to miss some food anyway; all of you are getting plump."

He rubbed their heads and scratched their chins until they purred. As he poured their food into the bowls, he spoke over their loud gulping.

"I would have been home on time, but I happened upon Xera. And she looked so beautiful and it was so nice talking to her. And I, of course, needed to walk her home. In doing so, I guess I lost track of time."

He scratched the back of Aristotle's head and smiled. "Don't look at me like that, old boy. Your food was only thirty minutes late. And you should always be a gentleman. You know that, Aristotle."

Ryder shook his finger at his cat and chuckled, turning back into the kitchen. Ryder pulled a bottle of water from the fridge, and as he waited for his leftovers to heat, his mind wandered.

I probably scared Xera today. I didn't mean too, and truth be told, I scared myself. I just couldn't get rid of those thoughts. Though Xera did a pretty good job of distracting me. She is beautiful. She wears her jeans a little too tight. I thought about ripping some of the oglers' eyes out. Even though it isn't my place, but still, I wanted too.

A loud beeping brought him back to reality, and he stared at the pasta in front of him. Bright red sauce and chunks. His stomach turned, and he pushed it away, no longer hungry.

Aristotle stopped in mid lick of his paw and stared at Ryder. Ryder shrugged. "I don't know, Aris. I think I'm going mad. You know I have nightmares, and then today I was sitting with Xera and I saw, I saw all this blood and feathers." Ryder gulped a deep drink of his water and pressed on his eyes, calming the onslaught of thoughts. He stared at the tabby and continued.

"Golden feathers at that. I mean, little buddy,

what has golden feathers? And I just felt so angry and so lost, and I just wanted to rip things apart and scream. It was only maybe a minute long, but that minute took forever. I probably really scared Xera. I know I scared myself."

Ryder sighed and lifted Aristotle from his place in front of him and cradled him closely. "I just don't know, Aris. Things are getting strange. Maybe I am trying to search too much. I mean, the freak that killed Mom, he's back, I know it. It has to be him, all these blonde women dying, it just has to be him. Maybe I just need to back off and take a rest, just do my job? I mean, I really want answers, but not at the expense of my sanity."

Aris bumped his head into Ryder's chin, and the man smiled. "Well, maybe some sleep is all I need. Shall we, little friends?" He looked to the other cats as they sat at his feet, and he stumbled toward his room and hopefully blissful sleep.

A glen surrounded him, and the trees that bordered it were tall and straight and made his heart beat rapidly. He was no more than 13 or 14. He stared at the looming trees on either side. The palms of his hand sweating, he searched the forest for the man he was to meet. He sat still, defiance licking up his back and into his closed fists. He

stared around him, waiting for someone to jump from the shadows at him. He reached up to touch the black eye that was already there. Tracing it with light finger, wincing when his finger touched a tender spot.

An older man stepped from the shadows, his face obscured by fog or something. Ryder tried to strain his eyes but couldn't see him. However, his body relaxed as he knew this man; he was a friend.

"Hello, my dear boy. Always on edge? Though I can't blame you. Who's to blame for that eye? Raphael or Emmanuel or even Hester?"

Ryder shrugged. "Doesn't matter. They look worse than me. They always do."

The old man sighed and settled to a nearby tree stump. "You know why you are here? To start training, but I must tell you. You need to learn to curb that temper of yours. You cannot always win wars with just your fists, my boy. Though you do a good job of it. Just like your father. But not everything can end with blood. You need to learn to curb that."

Ryder shifted and bowed his head, swinging his hands back and forth and clenching them. The older man motioned him closer. With trepidation, Ryder moved forward.

"You are a guardian, my boy. And to be a good one, you must…"

The man continued to speak, Ryder could see his mouth moving, but a loud buzzing began to creep into his ears, causing him to shake his head. There was something in the man's words about a Halfling and Ryder's last name, but that is all he could gather. The buzzing finally quieted enough for Ryder to hear the next part. He gazed into the man's face, felt tension and sadness on the air.

"You will hold the balance of power between both the underworld and the heavens and you will triumph, you must. For if you fail, we all fail. You walk the line between the heavens and the underworld, the last guardian to walk the earth."

Ryder woke up with a start, his alarm clock breaking up the silence with its loud, shrill buzz. Ryder sat up and pushed his head into his hands. He groaned and his shoulders shook as he wept.

I am tired of these nightmares and dreams. Things that make no sense to me and just torture me with their constant materialization. These nightmares… if I were to tell anyone how real they feel, how if you take away logic and reason they make perfect sense, not only would whomever I told put me in a lunatic asylum, but I would be losing everything, everything I have fought for and everything I believe. I refuse to put voice to such, such myths. Perhaps this is my mother's revenge for never believing in her deity, in her myths. Too much bad happens for there to be someone righteous pulling the strings. Perhaps I am truly going mad. To question myself, my thoughts, take away my logic. I am nothing more than scared, I suppose.

Ryder stumbled to his window and leaned against the wooden frame, tears coursing down his cheeks.

I have seen the worst the world can offer, felt its blade lick my face, and I lived. So, maybe that is finally breaking me. Especially now as history repeats itself. I have finally questioned too much. I cannot take it.

Ryder slammed his fist down on the wood and cursed. *I refuse to believe that. I refuse to let the evil around me break me. No, I will not let it. I believe in things I can touch and see, a man of facts. Not a believer of angels and dreams.*

Ryder grabbed the nearest item to him, his coffee mug, and he threw it into the wall and raged as it shattered. "I refuse to believe in dreams that feel real."

He knocked his books to the floor in his hasty movements, screaming at the walls. "I will not believe in fallen angels and gods. I will not believe that I am a savior and that I am good. There is too much evil in the world."

Ryder growled again and tipped his chair. There had always been questions that had no logical answers since the beginning of time. Ryder had simply thought the answers had just not been found yet. And even if it were true, he had fallen long ago

"I am unable to be saved, that would be a logical conclusion. Would it not?"

Ryder reached for the last statue that took up his tabletop and he stopped, his shoulders drooped, and he sighed. He rubbed his eyes and leaned against his wall, sliding to the floor and leaning his head back. He closed his eyes. He felt the first stirring of a furry head against his hand, and it followed with Aristotle sliding into his lap. He could feel the cat's ruined face as he ran his fingers across it and held his friend to his chest, his own limbs shaking in weariness.

Ryder shifted and chuckled humorlessly. "Look at me, Aris. I am reduced to a slavering, tantrum-throwing child. What would Xera think of me now? I do not know if I could handle such a thing as fear or disappointment in her face. Though truth be told, I am disappointed in myself."

Ryder opened his eyes and looked around. He ran a hand across the back of his neck and sighed. He rubbed Aristotle's ears and looked down. He could not admit even to his most trusted friend that he was falling in love with someone.

Ryder lay Aris to the side and pushed himself up on shaky legs and leaned against the window frame again. He stood staring into the darkness, soul-searching most would call it. Ryder felt a nudge to his feet and smiled down at Aspasia. He pulled her white form into his arms and cradled her next to his chest. She purred and curled into his heartbeat, licking his chin with her rough tongue.

"I just don't know, girl. I don't understand these dreams, my mind. Maybe I am crazy, but they feel so real, and it makes me so angry. Dreams should not feel real; they are dreams. But they also feel right as well as real. I have always known my mother broke some rule and that I was the result. But I never would have thought it was more than just the wrong man. And some rules are meant to be broken. I don't know, sweets. I just don't know."

Ryder continued to stare into the darkness, his mind on far-reaching things, things that he had not ever entertained a thought about. Things that were not logical, and it made him sick to his stomach to even contemplate them.

Chapter 19

Duff

Duff stood leaning against a brick wall. A cigarette dangled from his mouth as he watched Ryder's window. A sick, twisted smile took up his face, and he chuckled darkly.

"Look at him unraveling, throwing a tantrum like a child. Logic can only get you so far, fallen one. Each lifetime he has grown in thought and come closer to the edge. Perhaps this time, the last time, he will fall right over. And I will have to do nothing; there will be no battle."

Duff stiffened and sniffed as rotten and decaying leaves filtered all around him. Lilith stepped forward in a swirl of shadows. She placed a hand on his cheek, and he leaned into it. His heart hammered against his ribcage.

"Oh, my son, such pride for something you didn't do." She scraped fingernails across his face and down his arms, leaving gooseflesh in her wake. She dug her nails deeper into his arm, eliciting a moan of pain.

"Shows how foolish you are, stupid demon." She moved closer, hot breath sliding across his neck, making him shudder, but disgust rolled in his stomach. "Your plan isn't working, Duff. Only a few more chances and then I take over. And you will not like me to take over."

Duff's head jerked back as her hand connected with his jaw, and she hissed at him. "Are you listening, idiot?"

Duff gasped when he met the cold, dark, fathomless eyes of his mother. She dug her nails into his chest, long, angry slashes of red beginning to peek through the tatters. She stood and whispered tantalizingly in his ear, her voice husky like crushed velvet.

"Listen closely, son of mine. That Greer belongs to me this time. Your precious whore can have his mate, but he is mine. I have plans for him. His mother fooled me once; she will not again. A mother will save her son. I have saved you countless times. And I will get the Greer I most want."

Lilith backed up, her nails still digging into his flesh, but she peered up at him through long lashes. "And if I need to, I will make you fail. I bore you, and I can kill you too. Follow the rules, Duff. Keep your hands off the Greer. Tell your mate I said so as well. She is more foolish than you. Stupid, both of you. Keep your eye on the prize."

Lilith removed her nails and patted his cheek, making him wince. "Good boy."

Duff watched as she turned and disappeared into a flurry of shadows. His knees went out, and he slid down the wall to sit in the mud and water, his chest heaving.

I knew Mother wanted revenge but did not realize how much. Enough to kill her favorite son and my Tamesis.

Bile rose in his throat and he slammed his hand into the ground, angry at the tendril of fear he felt for Tamesis. Duff shifted and stood, tracing the claw marks that marred his chest. One last dark look to Greer's window and he to disappeared into shadows.

CHAPTER 20

RYDER

Ryder woke with gritty eyes and cotton mouth. He groaned, rubbing at the gnawing headache behind his eyes. He shifted, growling at the pain that shot up his arms and legs as he unfolded himself from his armchair. He looked at the late morning time then around at the destruction he had wrought on his living room. He sighed, and his body sagged forward.

"Well, I don't believe I am going on a jog this morning. It is far too late. And I need to fix the mess I made. Especially if I still want to join Xera today for lunch. I don't have much time. Maybe it will help clear some of the illogical thoughts in my head because surely she is a logical person."

Ryder pushed from his chair and cursed as

white hot pain lanced up his foot. He stared at the offending piece of porcelain, a glare on his face. Aristotle growled at him and flounced away, his tail held high in the air. Ryder sighed.

"I know, Aris. I messed up. I let my anger get the best of me, but I just…" Aris meowed and jumped to the table and sat with his back to him. "I'm sorry, buddy. The silent treatment, really?"

Ryder rubbed at the bridge of his nose and the dull ache there. He shook his head and looked down at Willow as she curled around his ankles. "I think a shower is in order before I tackle this mess. What do you think, Willow?"

He bent to pet her silky head before he walked away, leaving a trail of blood drops in his wake. The water sluiced down over his shoulders, dulling the ache that lay there and in the back of his neck. A strange yowling broke his thoughts, and he stepped from the bath to follow the sound.

"Aristotle? What's the matter?" Ryder stared at his friend, confused. His small mouth wrinkled back over his fangs as he stared into the alley outside Ryder's window. Ryder rubbed Aris's head and moved closer to the window. He leaned out over the edge and wrinkled his nose at the smell that pervaded the entire area.

"Ugh Sulfur and decaying leaves. What in the world?" Ryder covered his nose and slammed the window down. He took a deep breath and looked down. *Sulfur and decaying leaves? Like my dream.*

Listen to me. Ridiculous. There is no way they are the same thing. Just a smell. But then again, Aris has never acted like that, never been snarling in any time of his life, even when his face was all ripped apart all those years ago. He had simply scratched and yowled, but he did not snarl. Stop overreacting, Ryder. You need to clean this place; you have a date today. Just forget about it.

Ryder looked around and sighed, staring at the shambles left from his midnight fit. Ryder met the green eyes of Aristotle and patted the cat's head. "No need to be so disappointed. I know it's a mess."

Ryder gave a small smile at the cat's low meow as he jumped to the windowsill and sat looking down as if he were overseeing the cleanup. Ryder chuckled and bent to pick up the nearest book, sighing as he did say. He traced his fingers over the cover and pages, smoothing out all the wrinkles.

"Oh, Aris. What have I done? Look at my books, my statues, all my wood carvings. I have not lost my temper this bad in so long. I am ashamed of myself. Perhaps I wasn't ready to come back home so soon." He ran a hand down his face, rubbing at his eyes.

"Well, let's get to it, just standing here lamenting is getting me nowhere." Ryder bent to the task of finishing cleaning his living room, not paying attention to the time. He was thrown from his chaotic thoughts by a loud knock at the door. He frowned and walked toward it, opening the door to come face to face with Xera.

He glanced at his watch and growled to himself. 'Xera, I am so sorry." His cheeks grew hot and crimson, he rubbed the back of his neck and shifted foot to foot.

"I got caught up in cleaning up a mess, and I didn't look at the time. Let me just grab my coat."

"Don't bother."

Ryder felt his heart fall in one fell swoop at her words, and he looked down. "Oh okay. I am very."

Xera held up her hand, and he stopped. "You know I thought about just not coming here and just going home, but I really wanted to give you a piece of my mind. But now looking at you, I really just can't. You look too sincere. So what shall we do? I already ate while I waited for you. Which was embarrassing, by the way. So you could invite me in for tea or I can go home. Your choice, and I hope you pick the right one."

Ryder stared at her, at the spark in her eyes and the small red stain on her cheeks and the way she held her hands to her hips, and he looked behind him at the mess. He sighed. "My house is a mess, but come on in."

He backed up and held the door, his face growing ruddier with embarrassment. As her hair brushed along his arm, his skin grew large with goose pimples, and he smelled flowers.

Xera looked at the mess and then her eyes came upon the blood on the floor, and she turned around quickly, her hair whipping across his chest. She reached forward and touched his arm, her voice slightly panicked.

"Are you okay? Did that man that is attacking all those people, was he here? Is that why there is blood? Where are you hurt? Did he steal anything? Did you call the police?"

Ryder couldn't help it, he smiled at her concern, at the furrow in her brow and the panic on her face. He touched her shoulder and squeezed, trying to calm her down.

"No, no, Xera. It's okay. I did it. That mess is from me and the blood on the floor. I stepped on a piece of statuette. Really, it's okay. Though, truth be told, I wouldn't mind getting a piece of that terrible person. They are probably who killed my mom, and I would love to make them pay for it."

Xera stared at him, her mouth slightly parted. How he wanted to kiss the confusion and fear off her face. He shuddered at the thought and backed up, afraid that he would do just that and get slapped for it.

Xera shifted and crossed her arms. She stared at the floor and the mess with a raised brow. Ryder shook his head, looking over the mess again.

At least it's not as bad as it was. I mean, if she would have come just an hour earlier. God, I can't believe I missed our lunch date. I am such an ass. I really need to work on this people thing. At least she came here; at least she cares enough to check on me.

Xera cleared her throat, and he met her gaze. She gave him a small smile and shrugged out of her coat. "Okay, well, how about that tea? And you can tell me about this mess. I think I deserve that explanation, at any rate, Ryder. And perhaps you need to tell someone about it, because this…"

She held out her hand to the mess and frowned.

"This is the mess of a self-destructive person, believe me, I know."

Ryder stared at her and looked down, shame licking at his insides. "Yeah, maybe I do. Alright, well, this way then. I don't know what kind of tea I have. I prefer coffee, but I have some."

Xera settled at his kitchen table, cooing at Aristotle as he jumped to sit in front of her and the girls wound around her feet. "Aren't you just the sweetest things."

Ryder leaned against the countertop, waiting for the water to boil as he watched her interact with his cats. He looked at the pot of water. He probably could have microwaved it, but he felt it tasted better this way.

Xera held Willow to her face and kissed her pink nose. "Oh my gosh, your cats are beautiful.

What are their names? Where did you get them?"

Ryder chuckled and spoke softly. "The tabby in front of you, that is Aristotle, the white girl with the bright eyes, that is Aspasia, and the two gray girls at your feet are the sisters Willow and Diana. All of them were strays at one time. Aristotle has been with me the longest. He turns nine this year."

He held out his hand to the male tabby, but the cat didn't move, preferring Xera to him at the moment. Xera rubbed Aris's face again, and Ryder shook his head, mumbling under his breath. "Traitor." But he didn't really mind. It was good for his felines to get some love from others.

"Well, Aristotle, aren't you just the lucky fellow, surrounded by girls. And such pretty girls too." Xera continued to pet him as Ryder turned to take the water off the stove. "Milk or sugar?"

Xera looked up. "Just some sugar please, and thank you."

Ryder sat the cup down in front of her and watched as her delicate fingers curled around the mug. She looked up at him and frowned and looked through his arch into the bright living room beyond. "So, you want to tell me about that mess and why you missed our lunch date? I usually don't give second chances, Ryder."

Ryder shifted and settled into the chair across from her, holding his own mug of tea, though his was full of milk and sugar. He sighed and rubbed his forehead. "Honestly, you probably aren't going to want to give me a second chance after I tell you this anyway. I fear, Xera, that I came home too soon."

Ryder looked around at the little walls, the bright, gleaming surfaces, the first home he had ever owned, something that was all his. He looked back to her and met her blue eyes, expecting pity, but all he saw was sorrow and understanding so he continued, rubbing the top of Willow's head as she jumped into his lap.

"Well, I told you my mother died; what I didn't tell you was she was murdered nine years ago now. And we lived here. I moved away as soon as I could."

Xera reached across and grabbed his hand from the mug of tea and squeezed. "You don't have to explain. I read about it. I hope you don't mind. You had told me you were looking into your past, and I thought I would help."

Ryder's first thought was angry and betrayed, but then as he evened out his breathing, he coughed and nodded, realizing that it was nice to have someone to care. "It's okay. I wish you would have asked first, but I appreciate it all the same."

Xera blushed and removed her hand, tugging at the hair that lay over her shoulder. Ryder smiled at her and continued. "Well then, you know the guy was never caught, and he's back, or at least I think he is. I mean, the same thing happened to my mom.

She was just all cut up and, well, so was I." He traced fingers across the scar that took up his face and cheek, rubbing down it, his thoughts drifting to the days of surgeries, the loathing when he looked in the mirror, now just memories.

He cleared his throat. "Anyway, add that to the dreams, and I just sort of lost it I guess. I am so tired of dreams and bad memories and, well, just everything. I wish they would catch that guy and, you know, I am, or I believe, in facts and history. But I dream about angels and devils and creatures not human and, well, they seem so real and they're not. I know that."

Xera stared at him and shook her head. "Dreams huh? They can certainly disrupt your thoughts and your days." She frowned and continued, meeting his eyes. "Well, who says they aren't real? Just because you can't see them doesn't mean they're not there. And you want facts, read the bible, or the Koran or any of those types of books, or read even real true tales of miracles and angels and fate. I am sorry you are having bad dreams, though. I have nightmares a lot, especially when I take medicine for this leg of mine. They aren't fun."

Ryder watched as the light dimmed from her eyes just a bit as she talked about the nightmares she had. He couldn't help but notice the small sip of tea she took, the soft cast her face took on as she tasted and savored it.

"Not to change the subject, but what did happen to your leg? If I can ask? And I don't believe there is a god, Xera, or any type of being. If there was, none of this would have happened, the world wouldn't be a mess."

Xera smiled and shrugged, leaning back. She laid her hands flat and stretched a bit. "Oh, no harm in asking. But let me say first, I am sorry that you feel that way. You should have an open mind. My mother always said there's secrets in the shadows of the world and our dreams and we shouldn't take them lightly. And besides, good things happen too, a lot more than people say. But that is a tale for another day. As for my leg."

Xera looked down, disgust lacing her face as she squeezed her knee. Ryder wanted to reach across and hold her hand, but something stopped him.

"I was adopted at ten, and it was the most magical day of my life until I got home and I met my new father outside of the youth services office. He was not a nice man and alcohol and drugs ruled his life, but my mother, being the sweet thing that she was, loved him despite it all. Fast forward a few years. I was twenty-two, and my mother and I had gone out to watch a movie. Unfortunately, Darren didn't stay nor did he go home. Instead, he went out to have a celebration of his own. He came back to get us and, though he reeked of booze and other terrible things, my mother got in the car anyway. And because she did, so did I."

Ryder watched as her eyes filled up with tears, but she cleared her throat and continued. "It would have been worse for her if we hadn't anyway. But he ran a red light, and we were t-boned by a huge truck, my leg was shattered, my arm too, but my mother was killed and Darren, well, that jerk walked away without a scratch. It took me a long time to get better, and I had promised my mother that I would go to school because I always wanted too, so I did. After Darren was put in jail of course. I gave myself time to heal and to make sure he went to prison. Honestly, I hope he rots there."

Ryder watched her eyes grow heated with barely concealed anger, but she closed her eyes and took a deep breath. When she opened them, she was calm as could be. Ryder stared at her in amazement and smiled.

"I wish I could calm down that easily."

Xera laughed and shook her head. "Clearly you need to, but it took me a long time and a lot of therapy to be able to do that. Now, as much as I love this chat, how about we get this room cleaned up and try for dinner and a movie instead?"
Ryder grinned and stood. He held out his hand. "Or you could sit and pet the cats and I'll finish cleaning and then we can go out? After all, it is my mess."

Xera laughed and grabbed his hand, her smaller hand sliding perfectly into his larger one. "You'll take too long; you're a man." She gave him an ornery grin and stepped toward the living room.

Ryder stared at her and smiled, following her, his cats weaving in and out of both their legs.

Ryder picked up the last statue and stood surveying the now clean room, his eyes resting on the cats that laid on top of each other in the nearby window, catching the last few rays of sun. Xera stood and held in her arms an old, worn leather-bound book.

"What's this? It's beautiful." She held it out to him.

Ryder pulled it from her hands with a reminiscent smile and laid his hand gently on the cover, tracing the golden letters stamped across the top of the book, his last name gilded in his favorite color.

"It's my photo album, mostly the cats and places I've been, but there's a few in here of me as a child and my mom."

Xera looked at his hands and smiled. "May I look? Or are you ready to go?"

Ryder held it out to her. "Sure. I have to feed the cats and put shoes on, then we can go." Ryder smiled as she curled into his chair as if she belonged there, and he ran his hand through his hair, exultant that she had come today.

Ryder was lacing his boots when Xera walked up to him, a small frown between her eyes. He looked up at her and asked, "What's wrong?"

Xera shook her head and held out the book. "Do you know who that man is with that woman? He looks so familiar, but I can't even begin to tell you why."

Ryder pulled it forward and stared at it. And he shrugged though anger licked through his body, making his head hurt. "I don't remember his name. He was a jackass. He was my mom's last boyfriend, and he's the reason I have some scars."

He pushed the book back at her, debating whether or not to see her out. She was asking questions he didn't want to answer, questions about his life, questions that he couldn't answer because even he didn't know. She looked up at him and then back to the photo and closed the book.

"Well, I guess it doesn't matter right now. He sort of looks like Duff. But I know most of Duff's family, and I don't recognize him. So maybe that's just it."

She turned and slid the album back into the case where it belonged, giving it a gentle pat as she did so. Though anger still pushed at his temples, Ryder smiled at her sweetness. He scowled at the mention of Duff and spoke sharper than he had intended.

"What is the deal between you and him anyway? He's not very nice. And he treats you badly."

Xera laughed and shook her head. "If I didn't

know better, I would swear you are jealous. Which makes no sense. For one, he and I are just friends. He has a girlfriend, and you and I are only going on our first date. And yes, I suppose he can be mean, but he doesn't mean any harm. His mother coddled him way too much."

Ryder shifted and shrugged, looking away from her. She laughed as she slid her hand into the crook of his elbow.

"You know, jealousy does not suit you. And you needn't worry about Duff or anyone else for that matter. You are the only one I am interested in. As for Duff and I, I have known him since I was a child. My mother and his mother were best friends, amazing, really, given the type of person he and his family are. I always wondered about it. Anyway, he's the only friend I have here besides you. I am not very good at making friends. I tend to be a loner. Now come on, I am getting hungry."

She tugged at his arm, and Ryder couldn't help the smile that graced his features as he allowed her to lead the way.

Chapter 21

Xera

Xera woke up and stretched her arms above her head, a small smile on her face at the morning sun. She sat up and swung her legs over the side, smiling even wider as she thought of the day before and its perfect, though unusual, spark.

I had so much fun. Even though it started out so badly, it ended well. I'm glad I didn't talk myself out of going to see Ryder. He really deserved a good talking to anyway, but then when I saw him, I just couldn't do it. Poor guy feeling like he's losing his mind over dreams. I wish I could fix them for him, for my librarian.

Xera touched her hands to her cheeks, chuckling at the blush that stole across her pale cheeks in a red hue. She shook her head, both warmed and ashamed at her assumptions of Ryder and herself.

I can't help the hope of making him mine. I wish I could help him feel better, and I see nothing wrong with dreams. Mother always told me to keep an open mind, one of the many reasons I keep a dream journal. However, Ryder's dreams just seem to make him angry. I suppose it makes sense; he fully believes in knowledge. I think it may be his crutch from a troubled childhood. He is such a sweet man, though, and he cares so much about so many things and his cats. Look how many cats he saved. Maybe I can figure out how to help. Right now, though, I need to work on my history project. I only have a month left to finish it. And if I want to see Ryder later today, and I do, I need to work on it.

Xera shuffled from her bed, stretching her leg gently as she did so, the ache in it dull but still there. *Rain must be on the horizon again. I really wish it would stop. Well, I have old papers to distract me and then Ryder later, so hopefully, it won't last long or I will be able to ignore it?*

Xera ran fingers over the papers spread out on her desk, some yellow with age, others not so much, just a few years old. A project for history class, to write a report on anonymous good deeds.

We need a little more love and caring in this world. Maybe if I can show people stories about it, then more people will do so. That would be the ideal thing at any rate.

Xera grabbed her nearest paper and notebook and began to take notes. As Xera skimmed the papers, a photo caught her eye. A picture of a young woman took up the front page of the paper, her face so eerily similar to the other girls that had recently lost their lives. Long, blonde hair framed a small face, and large blue eyes gazed out at the camera where a small, reminiscent smile hovered around her mouth. Xera traced her fingers down the photo, her heart twisting painfully at the acceptance and also deep pain she saw in the woman's gaze. There was wisdom peeking out at the camera as well, and Xera smiled to herself.

What a beautiful woman, and so proud. Look at the tilt of her head. She looks as if she could take on the world, but yet so vulnerable and sad.

Xera moved her gaze from the woman's blue eyes to the name that adorned the small print under the photo.

"Trinity Greer, a photo taken only days before her demise." Xera covered her mouth with her hand, her eyes growing wide in her face. *Ryder's mother, it has to be. How awful. She looks so alive, so vibrant, and he cannot remember her? Nothing about her. How awful.*

Xera closed her eyes and continued to read, following the story after story of her death and Ryder's recovery. *How awful. They thought he had murdered her? No wonder he forgot everything from then. It was probably so traumatic he couldn't handle it. Poor Ryder.*

Xera found a photo of him, the hardened gaze

of someone hurt by so many people, the wound on his face still raw and open, not yet scarred over. There was pride and anger leaking out at her, but she saw too the raw vulnerability that his mother's death had left him with. The sadness that lit his pretty brown eyes.

Xera jumped as nearby her books fell off the small table to bang against the floor. She looked to the clock.

Oh my, if I want to visit Ryder I better hurry. It's already past lunch. I don't think he was covering the library today. Well, I guess I will find out, won't I?

Xera looked one last time at the photo on her desk and sighed as she pushed it into the nearby folder. Her heart broke for her librarian.

Xera reached his door and stood staring at the quaint white against the blue and couldn't help but smile. The small cottage suited him. She reached up to knock, swallowing hard to keep her nerves from making her turn and go back the way she had come.

She was startled out of her thoughts at the tall man that opened the door with a smile. "Hey, Xera. I was going to let you knock, but I grew impatient. How are you today?"

She looked up into his brown eyes and found herself at a loss for words, just taking him in, looking for the vulnerable youth that had looked out at her from the pages of her newspapers. She smiled and shrugged. "I am fine. I just thought I'd visit you and your sweet cats today. Barring there will be no temper tantrums?"

Ryder snorted and shook his head, shoving his hands in his pockets, something Xera found endearing.

"No, I think I am good today. I had some nightmares, but after what you said yesterday at dinner about being open minded, I am trying. I mean, hey, why don't you come inside? It's cold."

He backed up and allowed her entry, and she walked round him, laughing happily as the four cats of his came from all corners to see who was there and ask for pats. Ryder chuckled and shifted, closing the door behind them.

"They really like you."

Xera bent to rub their heads and backs, cooing at them. She looked up at him, returning his smile. "Oh, I love them. They are the sweetest things. Aristotle here is almost like a dog, it's adorable."

Xera looked up at him and saw a small glimmer of fear or sadness, she wasn't sure, so she stood, rubbing her hands down the front of her jeans and spoke to him. "Are you okay, Ryder? What were you talking about open minded and stuff?

Something on your mind? Or that you want to talk about? I know I tend to press buttons sometimes, but I do want to help."

She shifted and tugged at her hair over her shoulder, trying to keep calm while secretly hoping he wouldn't clam up again.

Ryder ran a hand through his hair and shrugged. "Nothing much to say. I was just telling you that I am trying to have an open mind. I mean, I don't believe in angels or, or God, but I will try to not become so upset about my dreams, enough to, well, destroy my house. I will try and approach them for what they are, just dreams." He gave her a sheepish grin and shrugged.

Xera chuckled and touched his arm. "Ryder, I think that you do. Not to upset you, but I also think that you are really angry and you have every right to be I suppose. I think that you just maybe hide that piece of you. And in order to control your life and the memories you do have, you just, well, bury it behind logic."

Xera held her breath, waiting for him to get angry, to start screaming or tell her to leave, but instead, he stared at her strangely and then dipped his head. He was clearly struggling; she could see it on his face and the way he held his hands fisted at his sides.

"Perhaps your argument has some merit. We will have to see, though, and I suppose I could believe it if I wanted too. I'm sorry, Xera, I just...

Logic is more my thing. And let's change the subject. I want this to be a good day. How was your day"

Xera gave him a small smile and a nod. She sighed and shook her head. "Okay, Ryder. And I am fine. I tried to do some research today on some of my other classes and got distracted, but it happens."

Ryder leaned forward, a small smile on his face, curiosity peeking at her from brown eyes. "Research?"

Xera laughed and moved forward. "Yes. I am doing some research for my history class. We have to research something throughout news for so many years, and I decided to try and find all the good deeds that were anonymous. I remember reading about some when I was younger, and I thought maybe if I learned enough and shared enough maybe more people would be willing to do good deeds. I don't know how to explain it."

Ryder moved around her and sat down in his armchair. "Doesn't sound hard to me. I think you explained it well. What's one that sticks out to you?"

Xera giggled and settled on the couch, the cats swarming to sit on her and garner her attention. "There was one, it actually reminded me a lot of you. I mean, there was no way it could be you, it's over a hundred years old, but this man saved a little girl from a fire. All she could tell the people was that he was big and had a scar on his face, but he was nice."

Xera looked at him, her cheeks warming. "And it just reminded me of you is all, and no, not because of your scar, though I am sure that was the first thing you thought of." She crossed her arms and raised her brow, waiting for him to deny it.

He chuckled and nodded. "It was. But bear in mind, Xera, I am no saint or hero, just a librarian. Please don't get your hopes up."

Xera shook her head and reached over to grab his hand and squeezed, his own hand closing over hers. "You think so poorly of yourself. I do not have my hopes up. I don't expect you to go around saving random people from fires or disasters or what have you. It's just that you are nice and I think if the occasion called for it, you could do that. Especially after hearing of some of your stories from the other day."

Ryder shook his head and pulled her up as he stood too. "Well, why waste the day? Shall we go get something to eat? Enjoy some more conversation over some food? Besides, I am honestly starving."

Xera followed behind him, giving each of the cats a lingering pat as they walked out the door

Chapter 22

Tamesis

Tamesis paced back and forth, the words of the prophecy going over and over in her head. She had just been to see the Seer Tynan again, anxious to hear the words, to make sure they were right and she remembered them well. Her immortality and life relied on it. She crossed her arms and bit her lips, unsure what exactly to do. She felt in over her head with Lilith herself now breathing down their necks.

I just want Xera's death, that is all. Her death and her immortality. Is that so much to ask for? It is not right that the damned one is sticking her nose into the prophecy and the death. I am the one that wants Xera's death, not the queen. No, the queen wants the fallen's death, so why must she mess with what I have? But why shouldn't I listen to the queen she has made me. I am what I am for her, but bully on that. I need to kill Xera. I must.

Tamesis bit her lip and looked around with a shiver of fear. She rubbed her hands along her side."I hope the dark queen is not near. My thoughts would have me murdered without remorse."

Tamesis shuddered again and returned to pacing, her arms crossed, a furrow in her brow. Tamesis stopped moving and stood motionless, the last part of the prophecy circling around in her head. "The immortal chain shall be forged whether by evil or fallen has yet to demand."

She tilted her head and rubbed her chin. She ran her hands through her hair and spoke to the silence around her. "Why would the Seer tell me I would persevere if the prophecy is worded in such a way."

A voice answered her. "Soothsaying is an imprecise magic. I have already told you that. And Tynan is my mother's Seer! So she will lie in favor of what my mother wants. Do you not listen?"

Duff stepped from the shadows, an overwhelming stench of sulfur and decaying leaves wrapped around his aura like sewage. He stood, arms crossed anger and beating from his eyes. Tamesis gave him a small, simpering smile. "What, my love?"

Duff lowered his eyes and stomped forward. "Don't what my love me, Tamesis. This is foolish; you know that. You should have picked a different woman! One that my mother doesn't already have her eye on. You have brought unwanted attention.

Do you realize that! The ritual calls for any woman with an immortal soul, and we have thousands of demons that fit that bill!"

Tamesis snorted. "I will win, and it has to be her. You wouldn't understand. It has to be her! I will not settle for anyone else. I will fail if it is not her. No, it must be her."

Duff slammed his hands down. Tamesis jumped back, and her eyes darted around the room, looking for the nearest escape route. "I understand, Tamesis! However, did you ever think that this is somehow my mother's plan all along? Breathe you into being to further her own agenda. If you were to exist, you would have existed since the beginning, not just now. You are a pawn this time around, and you are making it so easy for my mother to manipulate you and me. You have an obsession with this girl."

Tamesis shrugged. "I don't care as long as Xeraphina dies by my hand. Your mother can do whatever she wants, pull whatever strings she wishes. And besides, you are glad I was brought here. So what if I do? I just want her death. That is not an obsession it is a goal."

Duff laughed coldly. "Really, you don't think that it is just a ruse to make sure her plan falls into place. You are a backup plan, as I have always been. And that is completely irrelevant. A goal that you are willing to die for."

I don't care if I am a backup plan. I am getting

what I deserve, what I want in the end. His precious mother can have the Greer boy. It must be Xera. Xera and her precious blessing. Xera the favored child, the one to find a home. The one untouched by men's vile agenda and hands. No, she has to pay for that, and what better way than to assure that I, Tamesis Jade, gain my just reward, my immortality. Xera must die.

Tamesis took a shuddering breath and sidled forward, holding her hands out in front of her. She met her mate's broad chest and stroked the edges of his jacket. "Oh, let us not fight this evening, Duff. It smells as if your mother has already seen to your anger. Shall I fix it for you? Make the pain go away? I am very good at distractions you know."

Duff glared at her, but as she continued to stroke his arms and chest, his frown slowly softened and he smiled and shifted backward and motioned toward the hallway. "Gladly, Tam. But I need to bandage these cuts first. Unfortunately, my mother's injuries can't be fixed with a wave of a hand."

Tamesis watched him go, a strange glitter to her eyes and a cold smile on her face. *Such a fool, my mate. He thinks he is in charge, but how he is so wrong. I will win this war, and when I do, things will change all around. Of that, he shall be sure.*

CHAPTER 23

DUFF

Duff slid along the shadows. He had left Tamesis in a tangle of bed sheets, exhausted and sated, snoring the rest of the night away. He watched in irritation as Xera and Ryder walked back to her cottage hand and hand. The sweetness of their conversation made his teeth hurt.

I need to do something. I am never going to get Xera alone now, and I need too. I need to force her to push him away, or Ryder push her away. However, I can do no harm to Ryder because of my mother and Xera because of Tamesis. What can I do?

Duff shifted and shoved his hands into his pockets, holding his glamor on him like a shield. If anyone saw him, they must believe him to be human. He stared down at the clothes, the figure, and groaned. *I am almost starting to feel human, shameful. I need to stop this. Push them away from each other. Tamesis' plan completely relies on Xera being alone, and the ritual cannot be disturbed once it is started. But what can I do? Could I make him question his sanity? Just as he did the other night? Surely I can make his life so chaotic he has to.*

Duff snorted and walked back and forth, his thoughts returning to Tamesis and her constant yammering about the prophecy. He frankly didn't give a damn about the prophecy. Prophecies were nothing but lies told on silver tongues anyway. They were simply guess work and riddles. Especially his mother's seer on top of that.

Nearby, the smell of sulfur burned Duff's nostrils, and he turned to meet the eyes of a dark creature. His body the color of coal with obsidian eyes and horrifying features of the damned. His mother's little pet. He growled, moving into a defensive position, and the creature just laughed. A strange, coughing laugh and shook its head. It moved forward and held out a red and black blade in its hand.

"The queen sent me with Cain's dagger for your beloved."

Duff growled and stared at the creature, he crossed his arms and looking in distaste at the blade. "I told Mother we would get it."

"Ah ah, defensive one. Mother got tired of

waiting. After all, the days are creeping closer. Your focus must be here, on this. Think you can win this one, oh chaotic one? Or will Mommy dearest be angry? I would love to watch your blood spill and that pretty little thing of yours… I bet she is beautiful on the inside all ripped apart. It has been far too long since the queen has been able to punish one of her own. Here."

Duff growled and moved forward, but the creature laughed and held up a finger. "Ah ah, little son. You wouldn't dare hurt me. You would lose that coveted spot you love so much on Mommy's bosom."

The creature held out the dagger and shook it, a smirk on his face. When Duff took it, it disappeared with a cold laugh and whispered words. "She will fail, chaotic one."

Duff stared at the spot the creature had been long after it was gone. He coughed and shifted away, his long shadow crawling up the walls as he walked toward home.

I don't know if we will win this one. At least we have the cursed blade to cut the throat of Ryder's lover. We must prevail. And Tamesis will not fail no matter what Mother or her precious creature thinks. There will be a reckoning.

Duff stared at the blade moving it around in his hands. A whispering came from deep inside and he shuddered. The blade had turned many mad with its power. He would need to hide it until they needed it. He did not wish to lose his mind.

Chapter 24

Gideon

Gideon stood staring at Xera and Ryder as they walked throughout the day, chatting and enjoying the fairer weather. His friend Kavi stood next to him, his hand on his shoulder. "There's one of the queen's bastard sons. Duff is his name. I can smell him from here."

Gideon turned to study the fearsome features of Kavi, the lift of his lip, the penetrating stare, and he listened to the growl deep in his throat. "Oh, Kavi. So much hate for those of the darker realms? Without them, there would be no balance, no us."

Kavi snorted. "Balance, what has it gotten us? It has cursed my son and countless others. So many deaths all in the name of balance. Balance is the reason there are no Guardians left on earth, the reason there are so few even among us in the heavens."

Gideon sighed and shook his head. "They are deplorable, yes, but needed. We must have an equal weight of light and dark; you know this, guardian. Without one, the other would die."

Kavi crossed his arms and tilted his head, staring at the ground. Suddenly, he spoke sharply, his words cutting and harsh both from his anger and the abused voice box of his. "What is the point of this, Gideon! Why must they constantly be reborn and relearn everything about themselves? They already know anything about each other. Ryder could tell you about Xera in his sleep if he would put his damnable logic aside."

Gideon gave a slow, sad smile. "You are ruled by passion, your son by logic; they do not agree very often. It is his armor just as your passion is yours. He has to have something to arm himself against the world, a world that has been against him since he was born. You cannot blame him, Kavi. Just as you are a victim of circumstance, of fate, so is your son."

Kavi sighed. "Yes, curse our name. Good night, old friend."

Gideon turned to stop him, but all his hand met was empty air. He sighed and wiped at his eyes, turning his gaze back to where he had last seen his prodigies, and his mind wandered.

Greers... Perhaps Kavi is right. Perhaps they should curse the name they are saddled with. The guardians of the world, only mortals tasked *with an important and deadly duty. Born into it, they had no choice, none of them, both a curse and a blessing. So powerful, the Greers; it is in their grasp to learn everything and anything, and when they love... Oh, they love so hard, and if you take that away, they lose their minds. Cruel trick of fate and her sisters to task a Greer with a guardian or someone to guard, that they are destined to love. Every single time.*

"Traitorous thoughts, angel." Gideon turned with clenched fists to meet the three sisters of fate, their long, dark hair and the way they stared at him making his blood boil. They stared through him, not at him. As if he were not worth their time, a bug on a leaf, nothing more.

Atropos wrinkled her nose and gazed off at Ryder and Xera. "I tire of cutting their life strings. Why such sad face, Guardian? Does it not please you to see your little pets still alive?"

Clotho stared at him, her brown gaze piercing "You call us cruel, but yet we have allowed them to live longer than most. Just because they are reborn means nothing. They still have lived on earth much longer than any other mortals, even some of the Guardians."

Gideon curled his lip. "Guardians. They are Guardians."

Lachesis giggled high and cruel. "He is fallen, and she has not earned her wings yet. They are mortal, Gideon."

Gideon frowned and glared at the sisters. "They will win this fight even with you and your yarns. Despite their mortality, they will earn their immortality back, you'll see. They will win."

The sisters hissed, but Atropos turned to stare at Xera and Ryder. She shook her head. "Strangely, I hope you are right. Such blurred edges around these two even for us three. Trinity blurred the fine lines when she saved Kavi from shadows. Bore a child that wears darkness on his skin and deep within his heart."

Gideon crossed his arms. "What are you here for anyway? You have never shown such interest before."

Atropos turned and looked at him. "This is the last time, for which I am glad. It has been interesting to watch them all this time. They are a curiosity, and even we get curious, Guardian. You would deny us the right to watch and learn? Though I still do tire of cutting gold for them. They must die to be saved, Gideon. I hope you have remembered that. You love them too much, and it fogs your brain. Peace, goodnight, guardian."

The sisters snapped their fingers and quickly disappeared. Gideon stared at the empty darkness and cursed under his breath. "Such fickle sisters. Curse their Greek blood."

Gideon looked one last time at the two younglings, and he sighed. He bowed his head and, with drooping shoulders, he walked toward the library and a comforting coffee and book.

CHAPTER 25

RYDER

Ryder walked alongside Xera, his hands in his pockets and staring at her as she spoke, her animated nature bringing a smile to his face. *So beautiful, she is so gorgeous inside and out. How she lived the life she did, I will never know. To think, we lived so near each other but have never met. Such strange circumstances to have met now.*

Ryder watched as she grew quiet and her face drawn the closer they got to her cottage and the dark center of it. She was so lonely all by herself. How he wished she could just stay with him.

Ryder shifted and reached toward Xera, clearing his thoughts. Loose fingers gripped her shoulder and he spoke softly. "Xera, why such the long face? I'll see you tomorrow for lunch, and you have my number too."

He warred within himself, railing against the thought of any physical contact, fully expecting pain afterward as with all his life. It made him uncomfortable. Her need, however, outweighed his anxiousness, and he pulled her into a hard hug, breathing shakily as her arms tightened around him. Ryder shivered when she spoke, her voice muffled by his shirt.

"I'm sorry, Ryder. I know I'm being clingy, but even just for a night, it's hard to say goodbye. It seems so final."

Xera chuckled and released him as she backed up. "Silly. I know, right?"

Ryder stared at her, tracing her face with his eyes. He gave her a small smile and shook his head side to side. "No, it seems right. If there is at least one thing I have learned from my life, and even my dreams, it is that everything is fleeting, even relationships. So I completely understand and it's okay."

Ryder rubbed the back of his neck. "You're stuck with me, Xera."

She beamed up at him, and he shivered as the very air seemed to shift, and everything felt right as if it was finally starting to click into place, his life. He took a deep breath as the very thought rocked him to his core. He was in love with her; after only a few months, she had completely shifted his world and made him realize there was more to life than knowledge and logic and cats. Ryder squinted up at the sun and frowned and motioned at her door.

"It's getting dark, Xera, I would rather you were inside, the doors locked and safe. They still haven't caught that psycho that is killing women. There was another death just last week. So please."

He held out his hand, waiting for her to lead the way to her front door. He would stand watch until she made it inside. So far, it seemed the man did not break and enter, he met the woman and took them home and most were blonde, something that was in favor of his Xera, with her long, brown hair.

Ryder smiled as she turned and trotted up the stairs. He listened closely and after hearing her lock click into place, he breathed a sigh of relief and started toward his own home. His breath was frosty in the air and his heart lighter than it had been in some time. Xera took away the gray, and he realized with a smile it had been a whole day since he had obsessed over his dreams or his mother.

Ryder whistled as he opened his door, but his whistle stopped short as a strange sound met him. He shivered, his palms growing sweaty. He shifted, tilted his head listening. He drew a deep breath, and another tampering down on the sudden shortness of breath. It was a slow, keening yowl of fear and anger, and Ryder had not heard it since he had saved Aristotle nine years ago. He pushed the door open and sniffed, a strange smell of sulfur and sweat reaching his nostrils. The very air of his cottage felt wrong, strange. He ran his hands along the sides of his pants, the hair on his arms rising. His entire body tight and coiled, the muscles bunching along his back and legs. His fingers shaking, he grabbed the nearest item, a fire poker, and held it tightly in his hand, the white of his knuckles showing up starkly in the dreary light that peeked from the street lights onto his space.

The hair on the back of his neck rose and his blood sang in his ears as he drew closer to Aris's yowl. He clicked the nearby light on and gasped as he looked around his home He dropped the fire poker as he stared at the disarray that had been his organized safe haven. Everything was strewn about, blood-soaked fur clung to the furniture, and there was food and knick knacks everywhere. Ryder stepped forward and looked down at the crunch underfoot. He stared at the pale porcelain of what was once a cat figurine, and he growled low in his chest.

He searched for the white fur of Aspasia, as it was her blood-soaked fur he saw on the floor. Finding her in the corner, he rushed over to her and lifted her gently into her arms. She meowed softly, and he tenderly ran his hands along her body and fur, checking for any deep wounds. Finding nothing but shallow cuts, he breathed a sigh of relief and held her close to his chest. He stared at the walls and the disarray. His throat filled with lumps, his eyes burned with unshed tears. His arms tightened and he glowered at the wall. He had not felt this forlorn in a long time; even his dreams hadn't invoked such blinding fury.

"What happened, Aristotle? Who could have done this?"

He stared at the walls and the paint that adorned it, bright red bursting behind his eyes. "Who do I call, Aristotle? I can't call security or the police; I do not trust any of them. Many of those who were there when Mom died are still on the force, and we have a hate-hate relationship."

Ryder's shoulder drooped, and he pushed farther into the living room, he shoved items aside, studying the walls and area around.

"I suppose it wouldn't be too much of a hardship to call the police. I mean, it's been nine…" Ryder's voice dropped off as he stared at the farthest wall and the red writing on it. His breathing grew labored and his heart fell to his knees. He rushed forward to touch the words, Aspasia voicing her displeasure at the jolt. He traced them and glared at them. Their simple yet complex meaning, and the dreams that it touched on.

"You can save no one here, Guardian."

Ryder's jaw tightened and tears pricked at his eyes, and he fell to his knees. He stared at the words written on his wall in red and grew sick. He reached for his phone, his fingers weak and his hand shaking. He wiped at his eyes, searching for Xera, the only number that mattered in his phone. When he called her and her sweet voice answered, his heart skipped a beat and he let the tears flow.

"Xera, someone broke into my house. They destroyed it and Aspasia… They hurt Aspasia. And the words they wrote on my wall, my wall and it's just…" Ryder knew he was babbling, knew that he made no sense, but he couldn't force himself to clear his mind or his words.

"I'll be right there."

"No, Xera." But before he could speak, she had hung up. Ryder stared up at the wall and held Aspasia even tighter to his chest, her blood sliding down his own arms to drip on his blue carpet, but at least her breathing and heartbeat were strong against his chest.

What felt like hours, but was only minutes, Xera burst through his door and behind her labored the kindly, older librarian Mr. Hennessey.

"Ryder, Ryder, are you okay?"

Xera rushed toward him and held his face in her hands while Mr. Hennessey stood behind him staring at the wall. Xera looked down at the bundle of white and red fur in his arms and gasped. Placing a shaky hand to her lips, she lifted the cat gently from her arms. "I will take care of her, Ryder. Come on, you need to sit down."

Ryder jumped as a hand descended onto his shoulder, and he turned to stare at his mentor blankly. "Mr. Hennessey."

The old man smiled and patted his shoulder. "Now now, my boy, no need for words right now. That will all come in time. Come with me, come now. To your kitchen. I think we all need a very strong cup of tea or coffee. And you, my dear boy, need to sit down and then, then perhaps we can make sense of this mess."

Ryder followed behind the man meekly, his large shoulders drooping. He sniffled, the back of his throat still burning and the lump deep in his chest digging deeper into what felt like his heart. Mr. Hennessey pushed him into a chair and bustled about the kitchen searching for coffee and tea and hot water. As he got it all back together and began to brew, Xera returned and in her arms sat Aspasia, clean and purring with quiet sounds. She held the cat out to him and Ryder took her gently a soft keen in his throat as she met his gaze.

"Hello, my sweet girl. You look better already."

Xera kissed his head and settled nearby. "It was just shallow cuts. All she needed was a good cleaning and some tender love. She will be fine."

Ryder looked up at her and smiled and then back down as Mr. Hennessey shoved a mug into his hand. "Drink up, my boy, drink up. Calm the nerves."

Ryder took a gulp and welcomed the burn that

came with hot coffee. A small thing to lift the numbness that had begun to descend upon him.

To think, just twenty minutes ago I felt that all was right with my world.

Ryder's fist clenched, and he stared at the mug, his anger returning with a vengeance. *Why? Why does this keep happening? I start to get a little bit better, my life gets going well and then some tragedy comes and wrecks it. Why? How is that fair? Xera wants me to believe in God and angels when clearly they do not believe in me. If they did, I would not be here right now; this would not be happening. How could such things possibly exist? If they did, why is the world and my life so terrible! What have I done to piss them off because clearly, if they are real, I really made them mad. There is no other reason that I would have to go through such trials in my life.*

He looked at Xera, at her pale face as she watched him and Mr. Hennessey's questioning gaze. He set the mug down with a thump and stared at the wall, the glaring red of the letters peeking at him from the other room.

Mr. Hennessey shifted and touched his shoulder. "Would you like to talk about it? This? These strange words, they clearly have more meaning with you than the two of us can fathom. I can tell you are angry. So can the lovely Miss McCall, I imagine."

Ryder stared at the wall again and growled

softly. "What is to talk about? Someone came in and defaced my property."

Ryder snorted and a mirthless laugh filled his mouth. "They took my nightmares and made them real. Someone has to have a tape recorder in here or something. It's the only reason."

Ryder searched around, fighting the urge to stand and start flipping things over and ripping them apart. Looking for the machine that could record his words; somewhere there had to be a bug.

Mr. Hennessey touched his shoulder and squeezed. "Well now, I don't know about that, Ryder. What makes you say that? What nightmares are you talking about?"

Ryder shook his head and bit his cheek until he tasted blood, the metallic a welcome change to the bitter that had been there.

Xera spoke softly. "Ryder. Ryder!"

Ryder lifted his gaze to her face and blinked, waiting. Xera frowned. "Why don't you tell him? I think you can trust Mr. Hennessey, just as you trust me."

Ryder shook his head and looked down at Aspasia and gave her a smile, rubbing her head with soft fingers so as to not jar her. The cuts on her nose were clear for him to see.

Ryder jumped as Mr. Hennessey cleared his throat. "First, please call me Gideon. I believe the time for such formalities is passed." Ryder grunted in response.

Gideon tilted his head and touched Ryder again. Ryder felt like shrugging his hand off, but instead, he met the older man's gaze, and what he saw there was kindness.

"If I may, Ryder. I have not known you long, but I do know from experience in my long years of teaching how hard it is for someone who adheres to logic much like you, that you have difficulty making sense of illogical things. So, please do speak to us. Perhaps it doesn't make sense to say anything, to rather just think about it, but it may help you make sense in your own way, about the writing on your wall. That seems to be the source of your contention, unless I am mistaken?"

Ryder shifted and stood, laying Aspasia in Xera's lap while he busied himself with cleaning. He bit his lip as he formed his thoughts in order to speak to Gideon with some cohesion.

Gideon. His name suits him, and I like that better than Mr. Hennessey. Too many ses. He's going to think I am nuts. How can I even formulate half of what I want to say without him calling the asylum nearby and having me admitted? It makes no sense; none of this makes sense.

Ryder stood, still staring at the book in his hand, unseeing. Finally, he spoke. "You will think I am crazy, Mr... I mean, Gideon."

The older man chuckled. "I have been alive for some time, Ryder, my boy. Not much you could say would make me think you were crazy."

Ryder gave a humorless chuckle and turned, laying the book on the back of his armchair. He spoke softly. "For weeks now, I have been having strange dreams, nightmares even, I guess you could call them. Strange places from what seems to be the past, wings and loud screams. They make no sense, really. There has always been the same thing. I was in charge of saving someone, I was a guardian of sorts, which is hilarious, I might add. No one would trust me to take care of anyone else."

Ryder shook his head. "No one in their right mind would make me a guardian of anything. I have anger issues, and I have to have knowledge and logic to work and just, it makes no sense. And besides, I don't believe in higher powers or angels or, in this case, fallen angels. And I especially don't believe I am one, and to have my dreams written on my walls, especially when I have spoken to no one but Xera about them. And she wouldn't do this."

He motioned at the letters on the wall and crossed his arms. Ryder met the older man's eyes and was irritated by the small smile on his face.

Ryder scowled. "What?"

Gideon chuckled kindly. "I think you are wrong and that is why you are so upset. You say you don't believe in higher powers or fallen angels or guardians, yet instead of calling the police, you called Xera and you still are standing there with no intention of calling them either."

Ryder shrugged. "It's a known fact the police and I don't get along, especially in this town."

Gideon smiled again. "Yes, that is true, but that is not the reason you haven't called yet. Really, if it were, you wouldn't be fighting with yourself, trying to justify all of this with us. I think you do believe in it, and you are trying not to admit it. That is why you are angry more so than someone breaking into and disassembling your house and harming your cat. And above all else, I think you want it to be true."

Ryder shook his head. "That's not true. What do you know of it anyway? And even if that were so... No, it isn't so. Why would I want something like that to be real? Why would I want to be some sort of freak or something like that? See, I knew it. You think I am crazy and you are making fun of me."

CHAPTER 26

GIDEON

At Ryder's softly uttered words, he felt his heart plummet slightly. He would never make fun of the youth, not ever. Ryder was his friend. He thought of him as family, his own son in a way. He sighed.

Oh Ryder, even with the answers staring you in the face, you refuse to believe. You allow your logic to rule you. Perhaps it is in our favor that Duff is getting desperate as this is clearly a desperate cry for attention and for Ryder to leave, be gone. To drive him crazy.

"Oh, my dear boy. I would never make fun of you. And why would I not believe you? I have seen far too many miracles in my time not to believe in more than we. And who's to say there is no such thing as reincarnation? So many others believe in it. I can give you countless religions that do, even Christianity in a way. After all, was Jesus not the reincarnation of God in a sense, though they still both lived?"

Gideon's heart tightened at the young man's hollow laugh. And he was surprised out of his disappointment by the sharp intake of breath behind him.

He turned to see Xera framed in the kitchen, Aspasia laid on her sweatshirt on the table.

"Really, Ryder, you are being ridiculous. Stop hiding behind your logic! Your dreams were given to you for a reason. And perhaps they aren't true, maybe you weren't a guardian or an angel, but they still mean something. There is no dream anywhere that doesn't and to see the proof there in red and blue on your wall. It is staring in your face. You claim that logic and reason are your realms of expertise, well does that not mean proof? And the proof is right there for all of us and God to see."

She crossed her arms and glared at him. Gideon smiled to himself. *I will not have to give anything away as it is. Xera and her fierce nature, gods love her. She will make him see, just as she always was meant too. There is hope yet. Finally, hope is on the horizon, and we may just have a chance.*

Gideon turned around to gaze at Ryder, debating on what else could be said. He frowned. If they were not careful, Ryder could become unhinged. Each lifetime, every lesson would eat away at Ryder's sanity and overwhelm him, especially if he refused to allow them a little grain of truth in his mind.

Gideon spoke softly. "She is right, you know. Is it not truth that all truth can become fables?"

Curse these riddles and clues. If only I could just tell him the truth. It is all there right before his eyes, and he refuses to believe, refuses to acknowledge that it is true, or even that it could be true. When did he become such a non-believer? What have we done to him? What have we turned this precious boy into? He is truly a fallen now, so much like his father and in a way, so much worse. So much anger there under the surface, boiling, begging to be let out. Poor Ryder, my dear boy. You truly were marked, and it is unfair. I wish I could have saved you in the beginning. I wish the council had not been so hard on you.

Gideon studied Ryder, watched as his logical mind worked into overdrive. And how he was angry but did not wish to yell at Xera. That may very well save them on this night; she might be the saving grace that pushed him to the edge of sanity but kept him onboard until he believed the truth and knew it to be his own history.

CHAPTER 27

RYDER

Ryder stared at Xera, heat rolling from beneath his collar. How dare the two of them step foot into his house and tell him his dreams were real when they were clearly not. How could Xera, of all people, do this and act so damned angry about it? He chewed on his lip, fighting to stay calm while listening to her. Even if he didn't believe her, she deserved the chance to be heard, especially by him.

"So, you are saying this was all done by religious fanatics? They somehow got a hold of my dreams and twisted them in their own way to make it so that I believe in them?"

Xera's jaw dropped and she stared at him. She shook her head. "No that is not what I am saying at all. How did you get that out of what I said?"

She rushed forward, grasping his arms, digging her nails into his flesh and looking up at him. Ryder stared down at her, her blue eyes wide in her head.

"I am simply saying to open your mind a little. Not everything in this world is logical. There is nothing wrong with thinking that perhaps history and reality are blurred. Aren't the beings of the world strong enough to bend the lines? I would certainly think so. Even you know, Ryder, that all legends and myths have some historical base."

Ryder grasped her hands and tugged them from his arms, holding them in front of her. He kissed her forehead, forcing the burning of irritation down his throat. "This is not about myths and legends, Xera. This is about dreams I am having. Dreams are not real. They are dreams."

Xera sighed and crossed her arms. "No, Ryder. Dreams can be real, and I think yours are trying to tell you something. You know I have dreams like this. I carry them around in my dream journal. For both of us to have them. It is a big coincidence. And clearly, someone else is trying to tell you the same thing. She motioned with her head to the writing on the wall. Ryder turned to gaze at it, holding her hands in his own and letting his mind wander.

I cannot cross that line. I cannot believe that I am something I am not or that dreams are something they are not. Even such a huge coincidence. She and I having the same dreams. She has them in a journal, perhaps they aren't the same.

To believe in either of our dreams. It would ruin everything, everything that I know and love. It would destroy my, my safety net. Is that what is wrong? Do I want to hide behind logic and reason, because if I open that door, there is truly no going back and so many things that I have fought against will be burst wide open, and I will have to be angry, angry that the gods or the god have allowed me to go through all the tragedy of my life for nothing more than their sick delight.

Gideon spoke up. "Even some historians argue that there were some things that cannot be explained, that creatures and things existed and walked among humans. You know this, being a historian yourself."

Ryder glared at him and pursed his lips. Forgetting Xera for a moment as he eyed Gideon. "Say I were to believe you. Why would I be allowed or forced to live such a terrible life? Well, Gideon? Why would a god allow me to live this way, allow my mother to die and myself to be abused? I have the marks to prove that my life was no roses."

Gideon shrugged and spoke softly. "Even I cannot answer that, but you must remember, Ryder, in all your fantastical stories that you read, is there not usually a pact of some sort? Something has to be given to one side or the other to fix mistakes of bygone years? Perhaps it is simply that?"

Ryder laughed and stared at him. "So now my

life is a fantasy novel? I am the bargaining chip between good and evil as they fight for mortal souls and my parents based on my dreams are the main reason for my tragedies, because somehow, somewhere they broke the rules. Is that what you are telling me? Because that is what my dreams are about and you want me to believe them, both of you? Well, isn't that just beautiful."

Gideon opened his mouth, but Ryder continued, on a roll now. He clenched his fists and growled. They were not helping. "No. If that is the truth that you want me to believe, then explain to me what am I guarding? Why would I be a guardian? What do I need to save? Mortals? Why would the evil and good both want mortals? Well?"

Ryder shook his head and stumbled toward his armchair and fell into it, his heart heavy and his mind roaring. How dare they make fun of his dreams, try and make reality where there was no reality. His life was not a fantasy novel; there were no angels and mortals and guardians.

He frowned, fighting to keep logic, but the things Xera and Gideon were saying were starting to click, make his dreams and the writing on the wall make sense, and it scared him senseless.

If he were to believe his dreams, then Xera was his soul mate and he was her guardian, but why? And was Gideon the teacher that had been in his dreams.

He snorted to himself. *You are going crazy,*

Ryder. This makes no sense, so stop while you are ahead. Send them both away, or at least Gideon. I need to think.

Ryder shook his head and shifted, clenching his fists as he moved his gaze from Xera to Gideon.

He glared at the older man as he spoke again.

"Well, if that is the case, then by all means, call the police? I have some friends. Would you like me to call them? I don't imagine that Bryson would want to be woken in the night, but he would come if I asked him too."

Ryder looked up at him and shook his head. "No, it is all right. I have much to think on. And I need some rest. I also need to clean this mess up. Would you like me to see you home, Gideon? Xera, you can stay in the guest room tonight."

Gideon sighed softly and shook his head with a small chuckle. "No, my boy, I can make it home just fine, thank you. Good night, sweet girl." Gideon turned and walked out the door, patting the injured cat gently as he did so.

Xera picked her way carefully along the floor, past the disarray around. She touched his shoulder and Ryder saw her smile when he put his own hand on top of hers.

"I'm sorry if we upset you, and I know it may seem silly, all this, but I think that stranger things have happened."

Ryder chuckled and squeezed her hand. "Just find me the proof, babe, and maybe we will see. Hell, bring me your journals, let me see if they are the same thing. Then, and only then will I talk about it."

Xera smiled and kissed his cheek. "Let's clean this mess up and get Aspasia into a softer bed. She needs some rest."

Chapter 28

Duff

Duff stared at his hands, at the red paint that covered them. He lifted his gaze to stare at Gideon as he left Ryder's house, and bile rose in his throat. He stumbled back into the darkness and quietly threw up in the furthest corner of the dead end alley.

Do not despair Duff; you had to do it. You needed to make him lose his mind. He was so close to losing it already. You did the right thing, and the Guardian can tell him nothing. He must figure it out on his own. How can he do that if the Greer's mind is broken? He can't, that is right. He can't. So Mother cannot be angry. I cannot be to blame.

Duff stared at the stars above him and laughed harder. His body shook with silent mirth, and he rubbed his hands all over his shirt, making the red cover up the black that adorned him. He spoke to the silence all around him, justifying his actions to no one but himself.

"I had to do this for Tamesis. I had to get the Greer out of play, and I did that. I made him lose his mind, so this is good. Tamesis gets Xera and my mother still gets Ryder. Just because his mind won't be intact means nothing. He can still be used for what my mother wants, for her main prize of Kavi Greer. It is all okay. Mother cannot condemn me. I did my job. I am Chaos."

Duff began to walk and stumble toward the alley entrance, his steps labored and chaotic; there were not straight lines.

"Perhaps Mother will not know of this. Surely she cannot see everything, and I know she can't condemn me, but Tamesis…"

Duff slammed his fist into the nearby wall, leaving a hole the size of his fist, and he snarled to himself.

"You fool chaos demon, what have you done? You have changed the course of everything. You have possibly opened the door for the guardian to walk through. No, I didn't. I did what was needed. I know I did. I have saved us all. We will walk among the mortals again and take what belongs to us. The balance will stay intact."

Duff grasped his head, digging his claw-like fingers into his temples until he felt blood begin to drip. "Stop worrying, you fool."

Suddenly, Duff was knocked off his feet as Tamesis cracked him in the jaw. "What were you thinking, you fool?"

Duff stared at her, unseeing with a strange smile on his face. "I made him lose his mind, my love. I have taken the Greer Guardian out of the equation, paved the way for you to take the girl and the ritual."

Tamesis curled her lip and stared at him. "You were supposed to leave the Greer alone. It does not matter what you have done. Your mother gave you one order and you disobeyed it! You just told me to leave him be. Yet you turn around and do the same thing. So tell me, Duff. What will happen to us now? You think of no one but yourself."

Duff snarled and slapped her, leaving a red mark across her face. "No! I did it for you. I have just saved you. Been telling you for weeks that the fallen, the Greer, that he was going to find you. I told you there would be death, yours. But you sit there like an idiot. I saved you, I saved myself, we are all saved. I told you not to plot his death. I did not kill him. I made him lose his mind. Mother can still use him."

Duff continued to babble, oblivious to his mate's reaction or the tears that pricked her eyes. His mind was on other far-reaching things. He had saved them all. There was no reason for fury; chaos and destruction had won again, he was sure of it. He knew it. No one could stop them; they would win. Tamesis would have her immortality, and he would have his mate.

Yes, everything is falling into place. The ritual day is coming, and Tamesis has found the perfect place.

He rubbed his claws together. "Come, my love, this is all for the best. Come along. I am tired. I wish to sleep, so let's go."

He motioned for her to come and started toward the home they shared, a smile on his face.

CHAPTER 29

XERA

Xera woke anxious, her heart heavy as she thought of the night before. She turned her gaze to the far corner, searching for the basket that housed the simple white cat she had promised to take care of the night before. She smiled when she saw the female's white belly rising and falling. She was still alive, thank all the gods. She could not imagine Ryder's mindset if something had happened to Aspasia, or any of the cats really.

Xera shifted and sat up. She sniffed, smelling bacon and eggs. She pushed herself from the bed and followed the smells to the small, clean kitchen. She smiled, glad that the house was no longer in disarray. It had done much to ease Ryder's mindset. She peeked once at the wall and the letters that still stuck to it. They would need to paint over that, at least she thought so. Ryder was nowhere to be found, but a covered plate and a note sat on his stove. Stepping carefully forward, trying not to trip over the other three cats as they wound through her legs, she read the note carefully.

"Xera. I had to be at work. I'll talk to you at lunch. Have some breakfast, and I will see you later. Love, Ryder."

Xera smiled to herself and pulled the covered dish from its resting place and moaned in delight at the smells that assaulted her when she opened the wrap. She settled at the kitchen table and dug in.

As Xera ate, she read the old copies of the ratted newspapers that sat near her in her bag. Xera smiled to herself as she found a piece about the silent hero again, the man she had told Ryder about. This time, he had saved a child from drowning. She stared at the blurry photograph as he ran away, the broad shoulders and the wild hair. He must have been a good-looking man, but a giant by the standards of the time. The photo did not give her very much to go on being from the 1800's.

She looked up at Aristotle and frowned, laying her fork down. "I just don't understand how Ryder can say that God and angels don't exist. If there are miracles and people like this throughout all of time, then there has to be something or someone higher than that watching over it all. Oh, Aristotle, I know it is difficult for him, being that logic rules his world, but I wish he would just open his mind a little."

Xera tapped her fingers against the table. "And I am not saying that he is like a fallen angel. I am just saying that his dreams are more than he is acting like they are. And you know if he was a fallen angel, that wouldn't be too hard to believe. I mean, if there are real angels, why wouldn't there be fallen ones, right? And isn't that what demons are anyway in a sense? So then it's believable."

Xera chuckled as Aristotle rubbed against her hand, and she sighed. "I know, no use worrying about it." She gasped as her phone went off and, staring at the face of it, she quickly stood and placed her plate into the sink. She pushed the papers into her folder, unorganized as they were in their clear pockets.

"Oh, I'm late."

Xera quickly rushed to class and hastily slid into her seat before the first bell rang. She smiled as Gideon walked in, and she turned to speak to Duff but saw he wasn't there. She frowned for a moment, but before she could think on it, Gideon began to teach the class, and she forgot all about her curiosity.

CHAPTER 30

TAMESIS

Tamesis stood staring at Duff, her hand resting on the cheek he had slapped the night before. She curled her lip at him and watched as he downed one drink after another. This was his own fault. His mother had given him one rule, and that was to leave the Greer be. Instead, he had ignored her and done what he pleased anyway. Even after telling her to leave the Greer alone.

Tamesis stared at him, her other hand balled into a fist. How she wanted to rage at him, beat him and scratch him, but she swallowed quickly. The night before had made her realize her mate was losing his mind. This endeavor was proving too much for him, though she couldn't blame him. He had lived for eons, fought the same battles over and over again. That would tire anyone out.

She hissed at him, her anger finally overpowering the stay of her tongue. "I had it all figured out, the place we would do the ritual, how we would get her there and you, you have made her fall into her lover's arms, not push them away. What were you thinking?"

Duff shrugged. "We'll get her there, stop worrying about it. I told you, woman, I did what I had to do. I saved you."

Tamesis screamed and finally propelled herself forward to slap him across the face and arm whilst he stood like a puppy and took it. "You did not save anyone! You have probably killed us all. You went against a direct order and now to get her to the mansion it will take a miracle. You are a fool."

A soft, silky voice answered her, and Tamesis's heart plummeted to her knees and her chest grew warm with want, no, need. "She's right; you are a fool."

Tamesis turned slowly to stare at the dark queen, and she opened her mouth to speak, but then she began to choke. Tamesis grasped at her throat, gasping and writhing but being held in place.

"Did I request you to speak, whore? No, I did not. You have lost that choice. You will speak when spoken to and only then. I have allowed the two of you, you especially, you ungrateful whelp, the run of the world for too long. No, now you will do what

I say. You will do what I want, and you will not argue. After you have been properly punished, of course, but that is neither here nor there."

Tamesis whimpered as her throat opened, and she slid to the couch and hugged her arms to her chest and peeked up at the dark queen beneath her eyelashes. The she-devil strutted from one end of the room to the other, her long legs tightly clad in leather. The sway of her hips was tantalizing, and Tamesis could not tear her eyes from the woman.

Duff stood staring at his mother, a stupid smirk on his face, but he was thrown to the ground by the tightly-coiled whip around Lilith's waist. Tamesis screamed as the whip rose again and again, leaving long slashes along Duff's torso and on his face.

"Clearly, I have coddled you, I have spoiled you. It is my own fault. They say a mother shouldn't have favorites, they always disappoint. You have fallen flat from my aspirations of you, Duff, and for that, you and your precious demon swain must pay."

Lilith turned to look at Tamesis, and Tamesis quieted as the woman moved closer, she coiled the whip to her side. And she pulled a riding crop from the other hip. She traced the riding crop from the corner of Tamesis's eye to the tip of her v-necked shirt. She leaned closer and whispered in her ear, "I really have you to thank, Tamesis Jade, for this. You have ruined my obedient boy. You have turned him into a sniveling, cowardly fool. And for that, you must pay, and then when I put you back together and only then, you both will do what I say from now on. I will not be so lenient next time. Next time, I will kill you both. I should kill you now."

Tamesis froze and her body shook as Lilith snapped her fingers and smoke began to roll all around them. Heat licked at her insides and pushed outward, pain, unimaginable pain, licked up her limbs and down her side, and she screamed. When she looked to the queen's face, she saw savage delight light up her face and the two fangs that sat nicely in her maw glistened in the firelight.

Tamesis screamed again as barbed wire worked its way around her, digging into her flesh and tightening. Lilith snapped her fingers again, and they disappeared.

CHAPTER 31

RYDER

Ryder woke with a start and turned his light on. He flapped his hands down his arms and his chest, searching for the flames that had lit the area around him in his dream. Finding nothing, he sighed and fell back into his pillow and stared at the ceiling, his mind on the far-reaching things that continued to dog his dreams and thoughts.

"I need some air." He pushed himself upward and swung his legs over the side, bending down to gently touch the top of Willow's head, his mind drifting to Aspasia. As soon as he figured out who had hurt his cat, he was going to inflict so much pain on them, they would weep. He could possibly forgive defacing his home, but never harming his cats.

Ryder ran a hand through his hair as he pulled the coat on over his frame. Ryder stood outside and stared at the dark alleyways and the nearby shadows. He took a shuddering breath and, giving into the compelling feeling of movement, he started toward the center of town.

As Ryder walked toward town, his mind wandered to the night before and the events that had lead up to his stressful state.

I just am not sure what to do. I am at a loss. One, I could give into the dreams that Xera wants me to and actually believe there is such a thing as angels and demons and God or gods even at that. However, if I do that, it could end badly, because I know it will just make me angry, angry that they were not there when I needed them the most. However, if I don't give into such silly fanciful thoughts, then what? Am I actually truly going mad as I have thought for weeks? Neither side of this coin has a positive turn out.

As Ryder walked, his gaze darted from one dark window to the next, their empty faces behind frosted glass. A snaking tendril of fear slid along his back and into his hairline, making gooseflesh rise along his neck. He stopped moving, tugging at his coat and shirt, his breathing becoming labored and painful as he fought to draw breath. He leaned down, his hands on his knees and his head between them.

The dark. I never did like the dark. there is

something beyond the dark, just out of reach,
waiting, watching. It has always been there.

Ryder took another shuddering breath and
stood, wiping the saliva from moist lips, and he
stared at the open window face and growled under
his breath. Angry that he had been reduced to
nothing more than the panic that overrode him.

Ryder scratched his head and shoved his hands
deep into his jean pockets. He whistled to himself
and froze as nearby, a scream shattered the silent
night. Ryder looked around, trying to pinpoint it.
Giving into the instincts that tugged at the back of
his mind, he ran toward it, every thought,
everything, leaving him in the moment.

Ryder ran toward a nearby apartment building
and stopped short, his eyes growing wide in his
head. He covered his brow, watching as the orange
licked the night sky, turning the murky black to a
bloody tinge. He searched window to window,
looking for any survivors, someone that needed help
or the source of the scream.

A small woman with dark skin and brown,
curly hair tugged at his sleeve. He looked down at
her, tears tracing delicate lines down her face.
"Please, my son is in there. He is only eight years
old."

Ryder stared at her and then, without a word,
he ran forward, pushing at the broken-down doors
and forcing his way inside.

There's a child in there, an innocent little thing dying all alone. I will get him.

Ryder continued on, oblivious to the consequences of diving headlong into flames and ash. Ryder ran as fast as he could, searching the smoky atmosphere for anything moving. The scream further caused him pause, and he ran forward, pushing himself up the stairs, dodging boards as they fell and the flames as they licked the walls, consuming all in their path.

Ryder gritted his teeth, sweat pouring from his face, long, white trails falling down the soot that covered him. Ryder growled and fell backward into a wall as a beam fell and hit his head. He howled with pain and grasped his head, but he wiped away the blood and continued forward. There was someone other than him that needed saved this time. The frantic screaming grew closer, and Ryder stared at the door that blocked his way. Ryder stared at it with distaste and with a growl of irritation, he threw his shirt up over his face and ran full tilt at the door, busting it down with sheer will and weight. He did not feel the heat or the pain that came from hitting smoking timber with his body. All he felt was the overriding pain of knowing that a child was in there and needed help.

He reached the child and grabbed him into his arms. The child, throwing his arms around his neck, whispered against his shirt, "Are you an angel?"

Ryder gave a small smile and, turning, he ran

the way he had come. As Ryder ran with the child
in his arms, the debris and building fell behind them
in sheets of ash and timber. Warm liquid flowed
through Ryder's eyes, but he continued on. He
stared down at the child, his thoughts on the boy's
mother, and how happy she would be to see him. He
tucked the child closer and ran faster. As Ryder
placed the boy into the arms of the nearest fireman,
he turned and ran away from the people and the
cameras, his heart pounding in his chest.

Now, as the silence surrounded him as he ran
from the scene, the night's events came crashing
down on him, tears slid from his eyes, and his
shoulders shook. He stared at his hands and the
pinkness that came with heat, but there were no
burns or bubbles from burns.

How can this be? How can I be barely hurt
when that child was covered in burns? Is this a
sign? Or am I truly going mad all over again, and
this is all just a dream, another frigging dream.

Ryder stood outside his door, his sides heaving
and his hands shaking so hard that he could not put
the keys into the lock. He could hear the cats
mewling on the other side of the door, picking up
on his own distress no doubt. Finally, he slammed
the keys into the lock and pushed so hard he landed
in a heap on his living room floor. He curled into a
ball and continued to weep, the day's events and the
night before too much for his mind to handle. He
had just saved a little boy, but he felt strange about
it as if it shouldn't have happened. He did

something wrong again. He meddled with fate.

Ryder slowly gave into his nagging need for sleep and fell asleep on his floor, his door wide open and the cold wind stirring his hair, but he was oblivious.

Ryder stirred, tilting his head toward the sound of someone calling him. He shifted, moving his arm as something continued to poke him in the side.

"Aris, stop."

Ryder opened his eyes, speaking sharper. "Aris, I said stop." His eyes grew wide as he met a pair of startling blue eyes framed by blonde hair. On the wind, he smelled cocoa and cinnamon. He pushed upward quickly and gasped as his hand met bracken. "Mother?"

The woman smiled at him and then frowned, pushing against his shoulder. "You must leave. You are not meant to be here yet. They are coming. Hurry, go."

She pushed at him again. Ryder turned and tried to speak, but before he could say a word, the wind began to swirl around him, thunder turned the sky to a roar, and beside his foot, lightning hit the ground, charring it black and turning the air into a sweltering mess of electricity and a smell of singed hair. Ryder turned to run and fell to his knees, and the world began to growl louder and spin around him. He grasped his head and closed his eyes, screaming as pressure pushed on all sides.

Ryder lay still, his ears ringing. Slowly, noise pervaded his ears, the mewling of Aris. He opened his eyes and stared up at the ceiling and gasped.

"Everything was just a dream. The fire, my mother, the forest, it had to be. Why is this happening?"

He didn't move, but rather, lay still as Aris continued to press against him, his own furry body shaking in abject fear for his owner. Ryder pushed himself upward, cursing under his breath as pain lanced along his brow. He reached up to touch his head and groaned as his hand came away wet and smeared with blood. He stared at the scarlet color blankly.

Ryder stood slowly, his body bent and aching. He staggered to the bathroom, leaning against the walls as he fought to get to their clean walls. He made it and fell forward, hands bracing against the sink. He stared at his reflection in horror. Blood fell in drops of cherry to dot his sink in lines of red. Ash, soot, and wood slivers covered his shoulders. A deep gash, wet and angry, slid along his forehead. Four pairs of eyes stared at him in reproach as he cursed and stared.

"I guess it wasn't a dream. But then, did I do

something I shouldn't have done, and what of my mother? Don't look at me like that, I know she's dead, but I felt her poke me, I felt her holding onto my arms, pushing me away. Surely a dream can't be that real unless I truly am going crazy as I thought earlier. After all, what type of sane person jumps into a burning building?"

Aris yowled at him, and Ryder scowled. "Oh, hush. I know I have to clean up the cut. No need to growl me."

Ryder reached forward, pulling the medicine cabinet door open with shaky fingers, but nothing was there. Nothing more than his shaving cream and razor.

Ryder bent over, holding a hand to his back as pain lanced up his sides and into his shoulders. He grabbed the nearest item, a washcloth, and, wetting it, he placed it to his head. He groaned as the world tilted and skewed his sight. He fought past the bile in his throat, fighting to move.

Ryder walked slowly toward the kitchen, leaning against the walls again on the way through. He stumbled through the motions of making a cup of tea, something to calm the nerves that lay frayed and aching. He slid into his armchair, setting the tea down with a sigh and a curse as some of it spilled out onto the wooden table. He closed his eyes, ignoring the mess for now in lieu of pain behind his eyes. He winced as sharp pains echoed through his arm. He growled and placed a hand over the tattoo,

wetness covering his fingers.
I must have got cut there too. I'll fix it later.

The night time air that wafted from the open window lulled him back to sleep, as did the warm body of fur in his lap.

Chapter 32

Xera

Xera woke shivering on a cool, crisp morning in December, and she stared in distaste at the fire that was now nothing but ash. Grumbling to herself, she slid from the bed, crying out as her knee went out beneath her and pain lanced up her leg and deep into her thigh. She sighed and pushed herself forward, anxious to get the fire started and allow some warmth back into her small abode.

"I will make tea after I get warm. I hate to take the pain pills. But I may have too."

Xera turned her gaze to the window and stared at the dark morning beyond the windowpane as she waited for the fire to catch. She choked slightly when she realized it had been some time since she had seen Duff.

I have been so caught up in my budding relationship with Ryder that I have forgotten about my only close friend. I have been making more class friends, I suppose. I should really call him. After all, I did promise my mother I would stay in touch with him, allow him to help me if I were to need it. I could go to his dorm, but he has never told me where it was or even what it was called. Most peculiar. Maybe the school year proved too much for him. After all, he did flunk out last year, so perhaps he did it again. He was never one for learning. However, that doesn't mean I shouldn't try and find out more of how he is. I have been an awful friend. I could ask Ryder if he's seen him or even Gideon. Surely he would know. He's our professor, after all.

Xera glanced at the nearby clock on her wall and sighed, blowing her hair out of her face. "I wanted to see Ryder, but I guess I don't have the time today. I will meet him for lunch like always. I just really wanted to check on him."

She giggled at herself for talking to the silence around her. "Perhaps I should get a cat like Ryder. I bet he could find me a suitable companion. I need someone to talk to rather than myself."

Xera pushed her hair back from her face and bent at her door, trying to lock the door before class. She jumped when a heavy hand descended on her shoulder, and she turned in surprise to stare into the teasing eyes of Ryder. He laughed and steadied her with easy hands. "I'm sorry, Xera. I didn't mean to startle you. Though I am kind of disappointed you didn't scream, make the morning a little more interesting."

Xera giggled and glared at him, reaching out to slap his arm but stopping short when her gaze caught the hairline above his forehead and the long, red gash that sat there. She reached up and grasped his face, pulling him closer to check out the wound.

"Ryder, what on earth happened? Did someone come back to your house? Did you find out who hurt Aspasia? That is going to need stitches. You should have already gotten them by the looks of it. It will be too late now. My journals are inside."

Ryder paled but then blushed as she placed a small kiss to the injury. "Well?"

She backed up and bent down to retrieve the books she had placed on the top step, juggling them around until they fit perfectly in her arms.

Ryder shrugged and reached over to pull the books from her arms and tucked them under his own. "It's a long story, Xera, honestly I am still not entirely sure myself what happened exactly. And that's okay. I am in no hurry to compare dreams."

Xera stared up at him and shook her head.

"Okay. You will have to talk to me about it, though." She tilted her head and studied his arms, looking at her papers. She smiled when she saw the one she wanted. She tugged from the topmost book the newest paper. There had been a special edition out on campus that morning, and she was anxious to read it, see if she could use it for her news report for sociology class.

She glanced over to him, looping her arm through his. "What brings you my way? Don't you need to open the library?"

Ryder smiled and tugged her closer but nodded. "Yes, I do, but it can wait a few extra minutes. I thought I'd like to walk with you a little ways

"I am glad I garner more attention than the library."

She made a face and a dramatic sigh. "Sometimes I think books are more important to you than me."

Ryder chuckled and shook his head. "You would be wrong. What's that there that you're reading?"

He motioned toward her newspaper. Xera frowned and lifted it up. "I'm not sure. It's a special edition of the school paper. Came out extra early today. I thought perhaps I could use something for my daily news event for sociology. I forgot to look up a clip last night."

Ryder chuckled, and Xera fanned her face as her entire body heated in awareness. His laugh was endearing. "Shame shame, Xera." He teased her gently.

She blushed and shrugged. "Yes, I know. Speaking of current events, has Duff been to the library? I know you two don't get along. I haven't seen him in a week. I should check his dorm, but the only problem is, I don't know which one it is and, well, I am hoping it is nothing too terrible."

Xera looked up at him, waiting for the look of distaste that would follow her words, but she was stopped short by the caption of the newspaper's main headline. She stared at it, the words blurring beneath her gaze. She dropped her arm from Ryder's arm and looked up at him. She held the paper out to him, glaring up at him.

"Does this have something to do with your head injury, Ryder?"

Ryder looked down at her and glanced to the paper. Her heart warmed at the sheepish look he gave her, and he rubbed the back of his neck.

"I was going to tell you. I was, really. I had a few things to puzzle through first and, to be honest, I was just hoping it was a dream."

Xera frowned and looked him over, poking at his sides and pulling his hands toward her to study them. "Why aren't you hurt more than this?"

Ryder tugged his hand back and shook his head. "I don't know. That's part of the reason I was waiting to tell you. There's a lot of blank spots from last night, things that I need to go through. I'm sorry."

Xera crossed her arms and heard the first bell signaling that class was starting. She held out her arms for her books and stood on tiptoe to give him a kiss.

"You and I are going to discuss this later, Mr. Greer."

Ryder chuckled and pushed her gently forward, giving her a small kiss to her head. "I don't doubt it. And I will look into finding where Duff lives so you can check on him, though we are all better off without him."

Xera crossed her arms again and shook her head. "Don't be mean, Ryder. He is my friend regardless of how the two of you feel about each other. I told you, jealousy does not suit you."

Ryder smiled again, and Xera waved at him as she turned away. She frowned, staring down at the paper again.

How can Ryder argue that there is no such thing as angels and God when he should have died in that fire? He ran into a burning building if this paper is to be believed and he has nothing more than a scratch on his head and hands that simply look as if they were in hot water too long. He and I have a lot to talk about. I hate to say that he is a fallen angel, but someone or something is looking out for him if nothing else.

Xera slid the paper back into her book, her thoughts veering toward her religious class and what Gideon would have to say today. Maybe she would talk to him about this and see what he had to say. He was certainly more open minded than Ryder, but Ryder would possibly get angry. She frowned and shook her head.

CHAPTER 33

RYDER

Ryder touched a hand to his head as he watched Xera walk away. He had woken that morning with a splitting headache, a stiff neck, and aches and bruises all over his body. It was his own fault for running into the burning building the night before, but he found he couldn't regret that action. A little boy was alive because of it, and that was a good thing. It was about time good things happened around him, even if not to him, at least around him.

Ryder's heart beat faster as she walked away, her tiny, compact body encased in denim jeans and a light blue coat. It made her eyes really pop, and he tugged at his own jacket, waiting until she was cut from his view. She was beautiful. He rubbed at his head again and moved to his neck. He turned and limped toward the library and his work day.

I also need to find the time to talk to Gideon. I still don't believe any of this is true, but something is going on. By rights, I should be dead by now, especially after last night, and I have barely a scratch. He can't give me the answers I need, but maybe he can help. Xera's journals would certainly help. Though truth be told I am in no hurry to read them. I don't really want to know how similar our dreams are.

Ryder laughed to himself and shook his head, grimacing as he did so and the pain that slid along his forehead. "That was a mistake," he spoke to the empty air as he stepped into the silent library. He smiled at the fire in the grate and held out his hands to warm them, wincing at the heat against the pink of his palms.

He continued to speak to himself as he moved through the book shelves putting some of the books away. He held in one arm the fantasy books and the other religious studies. "I hate to think that there is anything but humans on this planet. However, something was looking out for me, or I am just some weird anomaly. And it's unfair, really unfair, that if there is something, they have done nothing for me. Nothing but turn me against them and kill my mother. Hell, I don't even know who my father is."

Ryder sighed and shook his head. He leaned against the nearest book stack and worked at a knot in the back of his neck.

Too many heavy questions on such a day as this. I need to stop worrying about it for now. I have work to do, and I need to find that fool for Xera. I don't even know about getting a hold of him. Perhaps I can call the advisors of the school. They wouldn't give me any information, but at least they could start looking into it too. Perhaps I'll wait and ask Gideon if he knows about it.

Ryder smiled down at the literature he carried in his hands and continued to move through the rows of books. He had until lunchtime to get all these done and then he would have some time to kill with Xera. Perhaps she could help him sort through his thoughts. And though he did not have her faith, he found hers refreshing.

He chuckled to himself and grabbed the next pile sorting them into categories as he walked.

CHAPTER 34

DUFF

Duff stared at Ryder, his distaste clear in the scowl on his face. He lifted his lip in a snarl and moved away from Tamesis as she leaned into him, muttering. He stared at her, at the cuts on her face and the long, thin lines of red down her arms and body. He sighed. His decision had been a grave mistake and it had cost his lover's sanity.

He growled and shifted again, his own wounds smarting and burning. He rubbed at the cut across his cheek, wincing as he pushed on a tender spot. His own mother had made sure to show him how displeased she was with him making decisions and how displeased she was with his mate too.

Duff moved closer, trying to listen to Xera and Ryder but stay unseen. He smiled to himself when he heard Xera ask about him. Even using his mother's plan, this could be a good thing. It meant she still had a little faith in him.

Duff turned away, and his gaze met his mate's. He traced the contours of her form and the scars and open wounds that now marred her supple body, the one that began at her collarbone and further down into her clothes. He shuddered. The things his mother had done to them, things that would never be forgotten.

He pulled Tamesis closer, and he tightened his arm as she stiffened, but she soon melded against him, mumbling at him and herself under her breath. He could barely understand her, and most of what she said was nothing more than gibberish.

"It is okay, my love, my sweet demon swain. Do you hear them speaking of me? It means Xera still trusts me. They do not know of my role in this cosmic plan. They do not know anything. The plan will still work. We will have your immortality, and my mother will regret harming us."

At the mention of his mother, Tamesis stirred against him and pushed away only to pull him back, whimpering deep in the back of her throat. Duff sighed and rubbed her back and her hair, calming her as best he knew how.

His eyes bore into the back of Ryder's skull. "I wish I could smite him where he stands. Make him pay for this. This is all his fault. His and his father's and those all named Greer. They are a blight on the land, on the ethereal plains, and they all need wiped out. The day the light leaves his eyes, it will be amazing, and I will be there to see it. No, my love, we will be there to watch as his fire dims, especially as you smite his precious bride."

Tamesis stirred and laughed low and maniacally. "She will pay. Precious Xera, sister Xera, she will die. I will watch her struggle to take breath and then plunge the dagger home. Daisies and daggers."

She continued to sing about daisies and daggers under her breath. Duff sighed again and shifted, tugging on his mate's hand back toward their home. She needed rest and he had some plans to make. Especially as the thousandth day neared closer.

CHAPTER 35

RYDER & GIDEON

Ryder sat with his hand on his brow as he researched the myths and legends around fallen angels, demons, and countless gods.

What better way to broaden my mind than to read about other things? Hard proof, that is how I will get through this.

Ryder dropped his pencil to the desk and pushed closed a copy of a psychology book about dreams.He rubbed at his temples, irritated by the nagging ache there both from the concussion he probably had and the memories that assailed him on an almost hourly basis since his brush with death.

Perhaps I just needed to be close with death to get all my memories back. Maybe the tragedy all those years ago blocked my memories and everything went away, memories and the like. Some of them were awful and painful, some of them happy, but all of them filled with some sort of lesson on faith from his mother.

Ryder sighed. He knew that his mother had made sure he was faith-filled all his life, and now, as those memories pressed against his mind, he felt beaten. His logic was failing him and he hated it, and he was angry, so angry that he had been forsaken. He tightened his fists and pounded them softly against the table.

I don't know why I am thinking like this. It isn't worth it. Her God wasn't there for her when she needed it most, and he sure hasn't been here for me.

Ryder sighed and stood, stretching out his neck and back. He stared bitterly at Gideon's closed office door. He had promised Xera he would find out about Duff and he still had to ask if he was allowed to call and ask about him. Taking a deep breath, Ryder walked toward the door and raised his hand, knocking hard on the wood.

"Hello, Gideon. Do you have some time to chat? I know you have to go to another class in a little while, but –"

Gideon held up his hand. "Of course. For you, anytime, my boy. Anytime at all. Come on in."

Ryder followed behind him and settled into one of the man's armchairs with a sigh of pleasure.

Gideon sat behind his desk and laughed. "They are comfortable, aren't they?"

Ryder smiled in agreement and then tilted his head. He took a deep breath and then spoke. "First, Xera just wanted me to check on that friend of her's. Duff? She hasn't seen him in a few days, and in pure Xera style, she is worried. I wouldn't worry about him myself, but, well, I'm not like her. But I thought maybe I could call around and get his information, and she could check on him herself."

Gideon sighed quietly and leaned forward. "You could call the administrative office. I can't promise you that they will you anything about him. All the privacy laws and such things. I haven't called them yet about him missing a few classes, but if they do not answer you. I will gladly call them for Xera and you."

Gideon leaned back again and met Ryder's eyes. "Some students don't last a whole semester. You should know that. Especially one who is repeating a year already."

Ryder laid his hand on the arm of the chair and nodded. "Yes, I know. But I did tell Xera I would ask."

Gideon smiled. "Oh, there is nothing wrong with such inquiries."

Ryder shifted and looked around. He ran his hand across his face and cleared his throat. "That's not the only reason I am here, though."

Gideon leaned forward steepling his hands. "Oh?"

Ryder chuckled uneasily and continued. "Say I were to believe you and Xera about this angel business and stuff. If there is a God, why did he allow my mother to go through such terrible things?"

Ryder shook his head and continued. "I realized today that my mother raised me to believe in a higher power. Perhaps that is why I have such a hard time handling that they might be real and not being angry. Especially seeing how my family and myself have been treated."

Ryder shrugged and leaned back into the chair and waited for some answers, hoping to get them while at the same time wondering if he really wanted them.

Gideon sighed and pulled his glasses from his face, rubbing at his eyes. "That is a hard question to answer I am afraid, young man. If you are remembering your mother's faith, then you know that many questions cannot be answered especially about those in higher power."

How can I make him see that it was for him without causing him undue stress? How can I tell him his mother gave up her wings for seventeen years for each of his lifetimes so as to help him on his journey? That his father would watch over him from the shadows of the world, keeping him safe? I can't and that is the true crime here.

Gideon cleared his throat and continued before Ryder could interrupt him and get angry. "I cannot say why your mother had such terrible things happen to her, but perhaps it was in the pursuit of higher things. Maybe she was helping others by sacrificing herself.

Gideon sighed as Ryder snorted and shook his head. "Hell of a sacrifice. They were still evil when they left, some more so."

Gideon nodded his head. "Unfortunately, that is usually the case. We cannot fix all those that need it or save all the strays. Even you know that. You save cats, Ryder; your mother saved people."

Ryder stared at him and blinked, nodding his head. "I think I will stick to cats too."

Gideon called out as Ryder stood to help the young man that had just walked into the library.

"Is your head okay? What happened?"

Ryder reached up and touched his brow, frowning. He gave the older man a smile. "I tried a leaf from my mother's book and didn't turn out injury free. Thank you, Gideon, for your help."

Gideon watched him leave, a small smile on his

face. Finally, Ryder was starting to broaden his thoughts and lean toward beliefs he didn't want to believe before.

Chapter 36

Ryder & Xera

Ryder hurried from the office, his mind still on what Gideon had said.

I suppose I should be proud of my mother for trying to save those who needed saving, but it doesn't make it any easier to bear. And truth be told, it was unfair of her to do so. To put their well-being above my own. But perhaps that is the way of the faithful. God and his words and message and jobs come first.

Ryder rubbed at his eyes, such heavy thoughts. He shook his head and held out his hand to the young man that had come into the library. For now, he would simply throw himself into work and deal with what would come later. He needed a distraction.

I will need to speak with Xera about all of this, make sense of it. Perhaps she can help me change things or at least change my way of thinking.

Ryder gazed out the window and then back to the student waiting on him. He smiled and started to find the books the youth needed and nodded his head as others trickled in. It was going to be a busy day.

Xera woke with a start and sat up in bed. She stared at the darkened room, wondering what had woken her and why. She saw nothing out of place, heard nothing. Then the knowledge of why came crashing down on her. She rushed from her bed and toward her desk, banging her leg. She howled in pain but continued on. She started ruffling through the papers that lay strewn across her desk, looking for all the dates of the anonymous heroes. Being careful not to harm them.

"Find me the proof, babe."

Xera covered her mouth with her hand, gasping into her palm. The proof was there in black and white right in front of her. She grasped the pages and laid them gently in her binder and strapped her bag on over her shoulder. Donning her coat and gloves, she started out the door. The wind whipped around her like a whirlwind, and the cold sliced to her very bones. Her leg was beginning to smart from both the cold and the banging she had done on the desk.

She knew that this could wait, but frankly, she was tired of waiting and of Ryder dancing around the truth. If what she thought was truth, if she put his dreams and her own together, there were so many strange things. She had always been open minded, believing that there was more to the world than most people said, but she had never truly been around it herself, and here she was. She may have found a great treasure in her boyfriend, and it was both elating and frightening if he was what she thought he was. Well, they needed to figure out some things. She groaned as her back grew achingly itchy again. It had been happening on and off for weeks. Just an itch that she couldn't scratch on either side, constantly there, bugging her.

Xera stared at his door and looked behind her, staring into the darkness around. *Perhaps it was foolish of me to come so late. This could have waited, but no, I want some answers and Ryder, he deserves some too. His thoughts and his dreams need to be spoken about. And this just proves it. He doesn't need my journals after all.*

Xera reached up and knocked on the door. She was surprised at the sight that met her and felt her cheeks flame against her cool skin. He wore low-slung pajama pants, patterned with no less than cats. His hair stood on end, and he stared at her through eyes half-lidded in sleep. The sleep pants alone made her squeak in quiet enjoyment. It was adorable. He was bare-chested, and the scars that riddled his body made her stare wide-eyed and unabashed. However, most of the toned body caught her eye, and the scars were second. She forced herself to lift her gaze from his yummy chest to stare into a pair of mocha eyes and a raised eyebrow. A smirk played about his lips, but he said nothing of her perusal.

"Xera?" He stared at her questioningly. Xera could see it there, the confusion in his gaze. She looked to her watch and tried to keep her eyes from falling back to his shirtless skin and the way he was so delicious looking half asleep.

"I'm sorry, Ryder, but we need to talk. You said you wanted proof, and I have it, proof that you are a fallen angel. I mean, add that to my dreams and your dreams and all this bizarre business, it really is the only completely crazy thing that makes any semblance of sense, even if it isn't something that would normally make any sense. And I am rambling."

Ryder chuckled and stared at her. He opened the door wider and stepped back, motioning for her to come inside.

"Come on, Xera. It's colder than the dickens out there, so get inside before you freeze, especially in your night clothes. And I need coffee before we start talking about angels and religion."

Xera blushed even harder and pushed him as she walked past. "Shut up."

Xera stared again at his bare chest and fanned her cheeks. She glared at him, at the eyebrow that was quirked above his head and the second smirk that played about his mouth.

"Like what you see?"

Xera slapped him again. "Shut up and go get a shirt on. I am serious, Ryder. We have a lot to discuss and, well, I would like to do it without distractions. What I have to say is weird and hard enough to get out."

Ryder shrugged and turned away from her. She watched as he ambled back toward his room, enjoying the view. She bent to touch the soft fur of Aspasia and kiss her pink nose. "You look better, sweet girl. Can't keep you down for long."

Ryder came back out, a long, white shirt on his chest, and he stumbled toward the kitchen. Xera followed behind him and watched as he pulled mugs and coffee from the cupboards, heating up the stove.

"So, what is this about fallen angels? I thought we already talked about this, Xera? I said I would have an open mind, but I meant about God and angels possibly existing, not about fallen angels, and even much less me being one."

He turned to look at her, waiting for his water

to boil. Xera lifted her gaze and met his eyes and frowned.

"Well, I know it's strange, but please hear me out. You said you wanted proof, and I realize you meant that you wanted proof that those beings existed, and while I can't prove that, I can prove that you are a fallen angel. Which is kind of the same thing."

Xera sighed and shifted, pulling from her bag the leaflet of papers that she had so carefully stacked inside the binder. She pushed it onto his table and gently spread them out. "You know how I was doing that project on anonymous good deeds right? Gideon has been giving me copies of the papers on these good deeds for months. Well, you actually gave me the last clue earlier today when you told me about going into that burning building.'

Xera stopped what she was doing and stared at him, putting her hands on her hips. "Which was very very stupid by the way. Why would you do that? You could have died or got seriously injured. It was foolish. Don't get me wrong, I am so glad that you saved that little boy, but there are professionals trained to do that sort of stuff you know and they have protective gear."

She pointed at his pink hands and shook her head.

Ryder nodded. "I know, but they would have been too late, but please, keep going, this is sounding interesting."

Xera frowned at him. "Don't mock, Ryder. It is unbecoming." She continued on, pointing at the papers. "Look, okay, these papers span over hundreds of years. And if that was not significant enough, they always describe the man the same. Tall and broad, a giant of a man with a scar on his face. And I know there are lots of people with scars on their face, but they are not large like you. And for that time and age, Ryder, you would have been a giant."

Ryder stared at her and then at the papers. "Xera, that proves nothing. It's crazy. I think I would remember being alive years ago, don't you think?"

Xera held up her hands and spoke. "Now, hear me out, okay? Add that with the dreams that you've been having and the dreams I've been having. And your amnesia."

Ryder stopped her and spoke quietly. "What do you mean the dreams you've been having? I haven't looked at your dreams. They could be completely different."

Xera stared at him, she sighed and held up her hands. "They are similar Ryder trust me. There are parallels, take tonight's dream. I dreamt about golden feathers and strange voices and there was so much chaos all around. And I've been dreaming of things hurting me, and there is always someone saving me. And you have been dreaming of saving someone. A woman that you can't see her face and golden wings are always covered in blood in your dreams, right?

She looked at him and watched in anxiousness as his face grew pale and he sank into the chair, placing his hands flat on the table while the pot behind them whistled. Xera bustled around him, pulling the pot from the stove and pouring him a mug. She shoved it in his hand and waited with bated breath, wondering if this would be the time he would scream at her.

She was startled as he stood quickly and started to move forward toward his coat rack, pulling the coat on over his clothes.

"What are you doing? Where are you going?"

Xera tugged on his arm, and Ryder held up his hand. "Hold on, Xera. Listen, I don't really know what is going on or even if I can believe this. But I think I may know someone who does, someone who may have known all this time. You can sleep in the guest room or my bed, I don't care. I'll be back as soon as I can and hopefully have some answers. Please stay here until I get back and don't answer the door for anybody."

He stepped forward and pulled her into a tight hug. She sighed as she melted into him, and he kissed her head. He looked down at her, and then he whirled around and ran from the cottage.

Xera sank into the nearest chair and covered her face with her hands. "Did I do the right thing?

Am I right, or is this just some overreactive thing from my imagination? And where is he going? Who could possibly know any of this?"

Xera stumbled back to Ryder's bed and fell onto it, Aristotle curling up next to her. She kissed his head and then, curling her legs under her, she fell into a restless sleep full of dreams and nightmares.

CHAPTER 37

RYDER

Ryder ran from the cottage, his mind spinning in circles. To think, mere moments ago he had been curled up in a fitful sleep. Though he wanted to laugh at the outrageousness of Xera's claims, he couldn't help but wonder if there was some validity to the statements.

It's hard to believe that she thinks I am a fallen angel, and unless she can prove it, I don't believe that it will really matter. However, for her to admit that she too has had dreams, it's hard to deny the similarities there. Especially with our dreams bordering on almost the same. At least tonight.

Ryder stopped running to lean against a tree. He stared up at the sky, wondering what he was really doing. *Why am I running? Who am I going to go too really? Gideon, because this entire time he was the one giving Xera the papers. He was the one talking to me of angels and demons and gods. Making sure that he made sense to my logical side, so surely he has the answers I need. And he will answer to them because this tomfoolery has gone on long enough. And if he knows the answers to my mother's demise, I may seriously hurt the man.*

Ryder groaned and looked back the way he had come. He stared at the only thing he could see of his house, the eaves, and he sighed. His mind jumped to Xera and her papers and her proof and he growled in irritation. He turned again toward the library and the answers that Gideon hopefully had.

He should be there. It's getting close to finals. He stays up late to grade papers. He even has a cot in the adjoining room. If he's not I am not sure what I'm going to do.

Ryder shoved his key into the lock and pushed the door open. Slamming the door behind him and locking it, he stomped toward Gideon Hennessey's office. He reached to pound on the door when it was pulled open by the man himself.

"Ryder, what on earth is wrong? You just barge in in the middle of the night. You're lucky I am here. Are you okay? Is Xera?"

Ryder surged forward, his eyes crackling and the plains of his face set in hard lines. He grasped the man's shoulders and squeezed, fighting the urge to lift him from the air or wrap his hands around the older man's neck and squeeze.

"Funny you should mention Xera. She is at my house right now spouting about how I am some sort of freak, some sort of supernatural thing, that I am a fallen angel. And somehow, she formed this half-assed opinion based on the sleeves of papers you've been given her for her sociology project. And similarities between our dreams. I want the truth, Gideon, and I want it now. You knew my parents or my mom better than you say you did, didn't you?"

Ryder held tightly to the man's shirt until his knuckles were white, and he stared into the man's eyes, expecting the old man to lash out, but what he wasn't expecting was the way Gideon seemed to shrink even smaller before his eyes. How his eyes filled up with tears and he offered a shaky smile.

Ryder backed up and let his hands down, rubbing them up and down against his shirt. He looked from one side of the other, wanting to just run away now and never look back.

He jumped and growled as Gideon reached across and patted his shoulder. "I am sorry, Ryder. Come with me. We have much to discuss. And I couldn't tell you anything."

Ryder choked on a mirthless laugh. "You couldn't tell me or wouldn't."

Gideon stared at him, a sad expression on his face. He motioned for Ryder to follow. Ryder followed behind him, his arms crossed and a dark look on his handsome face. He waited, shifting from foot to foot as Gideon moved around and settled slowly into his chair and pulled a tin bowl from the innards of his desk.

"Would you like something to eat?"

Ryder stared at him and snorted. "No, I don't want food! I want the truth. I want to know why Xera thinks I am a freak and what you have to do with it."

Gideon settled and rubbed his eyes, sighing deep within his chest. He shrugged. "I can't tell you. And she does not think, nor are you, a freak."

Ryder gave a bark of laughter in disbelief. "You can't tell me. What the hell?"

Gideon sighed and shifted again. "I physically can't until you believe in something. Do you really think Xera's idea is foolish? Or are you afraid that it is true? And if it is true, why would that make you a freak? Well? You, sir, need to look deep into yourself before I so much as utter anything."

Ryder took a deep breath, shuddering and painful. He clenched his fists open and closed, counted to ten. Anything to keep from tearing apart the older man in front of him for speaking in nothing but riddles.

"This evening, I hate riddles."

Gideon laughed and shook his head. "I am sorry, my boy. I know I shouldn't laugh, but you love riddles."

Ryder glared at him and snorted again. He held up a hand, trying to dispel the anger surrounding his senses. He took deep, steadying breaths, trying to remember the meditation exercises he knew. His mind, however, was blank and empty, and he wasn't sure what to do. He grasped at his head as it began to pound, and he tugged at his shirt. He began to choke, pressure pushed on all sides of his windpipe, and the more he tried to let go of his logic and his reason, the worse the choking feeling became. Then he actually began to lessen his hold on logic and think of things that had happened and were happening around him. Things that made no sense but made perfect sense, just as Xera had said.

Ryder looked down at his hands, at the pink tinge that colored them, and touched the gash to his head. By rights, he should have had more injuries, at the very least a small case of smoke inhalation, but there was nothing. Nothing but pink hands and a gash on his forehead. He growled as his mind crossed to Xera and the insanely strong pull he felt around her, the way she made everything right with his world. He rubbed at his eyes, prodding and pushing as scenes unfolded behind his mind's eye, of the dreams he had been having for weeks. Dreams about angels and magic and demons and gods. He touched his shoulder, tracing the figures of the flames that had appeared there, a new art he had noticed only hours before but could not remember getting.

He could not draw a single breath, though he did breathe out "holy fuck."

Then his knees gave out, and the ground came up to meet him as he fell to the ground in a heap. Ryder woke up a few minutes later to a cool cloth over his eyes. He stared up into the concerned eyes of Gideon as the man looked down at him. Ryder bolted upward, and Gideon moved out of his way quickly. Ryder's eyes darted corner to corner, wild and feverish.

Ryder touched his hand to his head, muttering curse words under his breath over and over again. Trying to calm himself, force some sort of semblance of normalcy to his panic attack. He grasped the bridge of his nose with two fingers and took deep, steadying breaths. He finally calmed down enough that he could speak.

Taking a deep breath, he spoke, "What the hell is going on, Gideon? I mean, Jes…sorry just what the hell? Seriously, I mean, seriously! How can I be a frigging fallen angel? They don't exist, and I think I would have noticed something like that, don't you think?"

Ryder whimpered as the thoughts washed over him, feeling like a thousand pound wave. Ryder brushed his hands against his shirt, brushing over and over again as he tried to calm his quaking thoughts.

This isn't logical. It can be true, it just can't be. I can't take this. It makes no sense. There is no such thing as angels, and I am especially not anywhere being holy enough to even touch one, let alone be one. No, this can't be right. It can't be right.

Ryder wrapped his long arms around his shoulders, his hands shaking and sweat pouring from his hairline to drip down his face. He traced fingers down the scar that lay against his cheek, grounding himself in the moment.

Ryder curled his arms around his legs and lay his head on them. He stared at the ground, blinking furiously as he fought to calm himself. He bit the inside of his lip in irritation and fought to keep from screaming.

Gideon filled the silence. "Are you okay, my boy?"

Ryder looked up, trying to focus his eyes. He shook his head and swallowed, trying to quiet the ringing that pervaded his ears before he answered.

"Am I okay? Of course I am not okay, Gideon. This isn't possible; angels don't exist and I definitely cannot be one. I mean, have you seen some of the things I've done? I am no angel, I assure you."

Gideon shook his head. "Well of course not. You are a fallen angel of sorts."

Ryder stared at him, one side of his face lifting in a nervous, twitching smile. "That's not much better!"

Gideon reached forward and grasped his arms, forcing him to look at him. "I didn't want to have to do this, my boy. No, I didn't. You have no choice; I have no choice. You must face the truth, or it will spell disaster for us all."

Ryder stared at him and tried to pull his arms from the older man's grasp as he shook his head. He growled as the ringing in his ears intensified. He jumped as the room began to grow lighter and lighter, and he stared at Gideon as the glow seemed to emanate from him alone. Ryder backed up and reached toward the knob on the door when a pair of golden wings burst forth from Gideon's back in a larger burst of light.

Ryder covered his eyes and leaned down, trying to shrink into a smaller position. He grasped the scar on his face and traced it, trying to calm down. He was startled from his ministrations by Gideon speaking.

"I am sorry, my boy. But I must say, clearly you believe it to be true, or I would not have been able to reveal myself to you. Even though you know me."

Ryder opened and shut his mouth, for the moment, his mind blank. He grabbed his stomach as his innards began to roll, and he bowed his head, holding it between his legs. He swallowed again and again until the feeling subsided and then he looked back up to Gideon but was unsure what to even say or think.

Gideon shifted, and his wings disappeared. Ryder gave a sigh of relief and leaned his head back against the bookcase, closing his eyes. Gideon broke the silence.

"I am sorry, Ryder, but this night is long from over. I imagine you just want to go home and think this all through, but you can't just yet."

Ryder gave a snort of derision and shook his head, still refusing to open his eyes. Gideon sighed. "I know this is all very much, and I know you are probably wondering why you can't remember anything."

Ryder opened his eyes finally and glared at the older man. "No, I am trying to keep from throwing up. This is an overload of information right now, and I am unsure if I have finally gone crazy or this is some wackadoo dream."
Gideon shook his head, and Ryder watched through slatted eyes as the man slid behind his desk and settled to the chair once more.

"Your dreams are the memories. Do not worry, you will remember more in time, over the next few days, possibly weeks. You are not crazy, and this is not some, er, wackadoo dream as you so eloquently put it."

Ryder stared at him and again grasped his nose between forefinger and thumb. He took a deep breath and stood on shaky legs.

"I am sorry, Gideon, but I just can't do this

right now. Please, I just want to go home and think things through, talk with Xera. I promise I will come if I have questions, but right now, I just want you to leave me alone. I have a lot to digest."

Ryder turned and slid from the room. He looked back once to wave but continued out the door. He held his arms stiffly at his sides, taking all his control to keep from bolting from the library. As he burst into the cool night air, he leaned against the wall and threw up.

He leaned against the brick and slid down the side to sit in the cool, wet ground. He buried his hands in his face and he wept. The logic that had long been his shield was no more, and he found he felt adrift and anxious. Sweat poured from his head and neck and his stomach continued to ache and turn.

This can't be happening. I can't be all these things, but the golden wings... Golden wings burst from his back, and he told me it was all alike, everything I have tried to learn and follow all these years naught but lies.

Ryder brushed at his eyes angrily, furious that he had been reduced to tears. He stood up and brushed at his clothes. Turning once to look at the tall library, he took a deep breath and started to walk home, formulating his thoughts as he did so and what he would say to Xera.

Ryder stood outside his cottage, staring at the door and the small lights in his windows. He pushed the pieces of his dreams and the small nuggets of strange memories to form a cohesive story of his life, or in this case, all his lives

I was punished for something. That would be the only reason I am a fallen, but for what? Was it because my parents somehow broke some kind of rules or pact between themselves and Lilith? For that matter, why would they make such a pact with the queen of the damned anyway? And why would I get in trouble for love, because clearly if my dreams are truth, I should not have fallen in love, but how can you stop that? But Gideon said I wasn't exactly a fallen, and I don't have wings like him. So what, am I a mortal? A demon since I am a fallen or am I an angel or am I all three? How can I be all three?

Chapter 38

Xera

Xera woke at the sound of a key turning in the lock. She stared around her, trying to gather her bearings and figure out where she was. As she slowly allowed her eyes to adjust and she felt no less than four furry bodies against her, she realized she was not at her own home, but rather, at Ryder's.

Ugh, what happened? What have I done? I accused Ryder of being a fallen angel. I was so certain, though, but now perhaps I was wrong. Maybe my dreams just have me all in a tizzy and I was worried about Ryder. And I wanted him to believe in something more than himself, more than all of us, so badly. I will just have to tell him I'm sorry and go from there.

Xera heard his call coming from the front of the

cottage. Gently removing herself from the bundle of furry bodies, she slid out into the hallway and farther down the hall. She threw her arms around him, and she was about to speak, but she caught sight of his face. She touched his cheeks and stared at the red-rimmed eyes and the way he held himself stiff and closed off as if there was something drastic that had happened.

"Ryder, are you okay? Where did you go? Who did you go to see? I was so worried. I am sorry if I upset you, and I know."

Ryder backed up and stared at her. Xera hugged her arms to herself, feeling a sudden burst of cold from his absence.

Ryder stepped forward and kissed her head. "I love you, Xera. But you need to sit down."

Xera stared up at him, and she pursed her lips and nodded. "Love you too, but that doesn't answer my questions."

Ryder shook his head and tugged her hand from her shoulder and pulled her toward the kitchen. He placed a mug of lukewarm tea on the table and motioned for her to sit down.

"All in good time, Xera. Please sit. And take a drink, I have got to make sure you are awake for this."

Xera slid into her seat and held the mug fast with both hands. She took a sip and then stared at him, waiting for him to start speaking.

"First of all, I am not okay. I honestly don't know when I will be okay. It has been an interesting night. And I went to the library."

Xera stared at him. "You went to read about things while I sat here worrying that I upset you?"

Ryder shook his head no. "No, I went to see Gideon. I figured if anyone had answers, he would. Not only was he the one that gave you the papers, but he was also the one that, besides you, really pushed the issue of angels, demons, and God."

Xera set her mug down heavily. "Did he give you answers? What is going on? Was I, was I right?"

Xera clutched her hands into her lap, squeezing the palms together, anxious and afraid of his answer. Beads of sweat dripped down her back, making her back itch crazier than it had been, and she moved around in her chair, searching for a comfortable position.

"Yes, you are right. At least, I think so. Like I said, it's been an interesting night. You know, Gideon has golden wings, these huge, large golden wings."

Xera stared at him as he stretched his arms out, a look of bewilderment on his face. "I just don't know, Xera. It still, just, it doesn't make sense, but at the same time…" He dropped off and Xera stood and slid around the table to lay her hand on top of his and squeeze.

"I think that all things are possible, Ryder. So this doesn't surprise me as it does you. There are dark things in the world; it is the only reason for some of the things that happen. So why wouldn't there be good things too and in-between things?"

Ryder shook his head and slid an arm around her waist. "You certainly are handling this better than I did. I am pretty sure I almost had a heart attack, and I threw up. I am still unsure about all of this. I mean, I am no angel."

Xera chuckled and shrugged. "Yes, you are. You just needed the proof."

Xera looked around and yawned. "I am sorry, I wish I could help you more, be more shocked and anxious, but it just can't happen. This doesn't surprise me. I think I always knew there was something otherworldly about you, Ryder Greer, and I just needed you to see it too."

Ryder smiled sadly. "Great, even you knew I was a freak."

Xera gasped and pulled backward, looking up at him. "You are nothing of the kind. You are wonderful and amazing and you shouldn't say such things. You are no freak, Ryder. I mean, I wouldn't tell people about this, but I would not say you were a freak. You are an angel. People would pay to be one or even to know one."

She hugged him, squeezing him tightly and brushing her hands along his arms. "Come now. I think maybe you need some sleep. I already slept a bit, so I'll clean this up. You go sleep with the cats. You need it. I will stay with you tomorrow too if you like."

Ryder kissed her forehead. "I would like that very much, thank you."

Xera watched him walk back down the hall. She held her left wrist in her right hand and frowned at the droop in his shoulders.

Poor Ryder. So much he has been thrown at today. All his logic has been stripped away, his shields forced down.

Xera touched a finger to her lip and sighed. She stared down at the one cat that had followed her, Aspasia, and lifted her gently into her arms. "I just don't know, Aspasia. All the lore I have ever read say they are a fallen for a reason. So what did he do that was so wrong? And how can we fix it? How can we make him whole again, sweet girl?"

Xera lay the cat gently to the floor and bustled about the kitchen, cleaning up the dishes and allowing her mind to wander. She and Ryder had much to speak about tomorrow and the next few days. Maybe she could help him figure it out. Give him some logic to stand on. To tear it all away seemed unnecessarily cruel and that was what it seemed Gideon had done.

CHAPTER 39

RYDER & XERA

Ryder shifted and turned the collar of his jacket up as he stared at the broken-down mansion in front of him. He scratched his cheek and studied the hull of a burned-out husk, gazing at the tall draperies that no longer had windows to hang in. The dark ash stuck to the white stone and was a wound on the precious landscape of beyond.

How terrible it is to mar such beauty, not only with the house too large for one's family, but also to burn it to the ground and then use it as practice for the firefighters. It seems unfair to kill such beauty. But then again, perhaps it is nothing more than justice for those ruled by greed. To lose their material items.

Ryder shifted and cocked his head to the side. He ran his hands through his hair and let his mind wander further to the enlightened thinking that had started to pervade his senses and his thoughts.

Ever since that night in the library when all was laid bare, the truth blown wide for me to see. I have been searching and have found nothing. No reason to the dreams and the memories. I have been alive for eons and died numerous times, but yet, I do not fully know why. Those thoughts, they are there, just beyond my grasp, and it is maddening.

Ryder crossed his arms and scuffed his toe along the frost, staring at the white against the shadows, a startling contrast to the darkness. He scowled as his thoughts continued to circle.

I wish I could accept this as easily as Xera did. It has been days, a week, and she has not asked questions or questioned that I am what I am in anyway. When I myself have questioned every day and then questioned even more. I suppose it is my logic again trying to root itself into my new reality. I know that there is evil around, that they are after Xera and myself. I know that there was something broken both by my parents and by Xera and me, but the details evade me. The memories are there, coming in slow motion, a few trickling in throughout the days, but Xera has nothing, none. Her memories are still gone, and I know that she is just as I am. Gideon told her so. He himself is a guardian angel, so he would know. But why can I remember and she can't and does that have something to do with this darkness, this foreboding in the air?

So lost in his thoughts Ryder did not hear Xera as she snuck up on him. Ryder stiffened as a sweet voice called out to him.

"Ryder, my love? Are you still searching the darkness for answers to all your questions? Gideon told you it would all come in time. We will find out what the evil pressing on all sides is, we will."

Ryder shifted and stared at the mansion again. "I just don't know. Something seems so wrong. I feel like we are on a time constraint."

Ryder turned and looked to her, tossing an arm around her shoulder and pulling her into a tight hug. "I still don't quite get how you can be so easy about all this. I am still reeling and you are just fine as can be about it all."

Xera shrugged and Ryder shook his head, kissing her head. "It's so ugly, but also so beautiful isn't it."

Xera snuggled into Ryder's embrace. She chuckled and spoke quietly, fearful that her words would disturb the silence.

"I've already told you, Ryder. The otherworldly doesn't bother me. I've always known deep down that there was more to all of us. There has to be more than what we know in this world. And why couldn't there be angels and demons and gods? Someone had to make the first person or creature you know."

Xera stared at the mansion he pointed out and pursed her lips. "Well, I don't know, Ryder. I think it was very beautiful once, and the landscape is still gorgeous, but the mansion itself... It is more desolate. It seems so isolated and lonely, and, well, creepy."

Xera rubbed her arms, the goose flesh that rose along them making her shudder. She shifted and blew on her hands, warming them inside her gloves. She peeked up at him and said quietly, "You should stop doing this, Ryder. Stop moving around at night and driving yourself mad with need and questions. Gideon said it would come in time. It will, you just need time to adjust; your logical brain needs time to adjust."

Xera traced his face with her gaze, trying to see beyond the impenetrable wall he had been putting up lately.

So brooding; he has become so brooding. I worry about him constantly searching for evil. I wish I could fix it all. And I know very well that this whole thing is so hard to take, and he is right. Honestly, I should be taking this much harder than I am. Most normal people would, but it just seems so right to me. It makes such perfect sense.

Xera sighed and shook her head, trying to dispel such thoughts.

He is so bent on revenge that I feel like I am losing him. He doesn't even know what he wants revenge for, or why. Just that he does. He is so stuck in the past that he cannot move into the future. I just don't know.

Ryder shifted and looked down at her. "Xera, I am a man of action. I just can't sit and let the answers come to all my questions. I try and it just makes my head spin, and then I get angry, and I hate being angry. I destroy things."

Xera snorted at his words and shook her head. "I can't argue with that."

Ryder glared at her. "Oh hush."

Xera reached to touch his arm, and she squeezed, leaning into him again. "I understand. I do, Ryder, but this is going to drive you crazy. Sometimes it is just better to let things come in their own time. You know that, right? Sometimes when you push and push, some things push back and it gets ugly. Besides, you have no idea still who did that to your house. It had to be someone or something that knows what or, well, who you are."

Ryder frowned. "I know, but just sit and let it come to me isn't really something I can handle."

Xera huffed. "You are so stubborn. Fine. By all means, let us just stand in the cold and freeze while we wait for the answers to come to you. What is the difference between being out at night in the cold versus being at home in the warmth, staring out the window into darkness."

"You didn't have to come, Xera." He chuckled at her and grabbing her hand. He pulled her off into a walk of the night air.

"Let's keep moving. It will keep you warm."

Xera held tight to his hand, grumbling under her breath at him, about the cold and the dark. *I suppose she is right, but there is something that draws me to it. The darkness has a secret in it, and if I am in it long enough, perhaps I can learn more about me, about our life, about the evil that is here. Gideon has not been able to tell me much of what is happening, just suspicions and thoughts.*

"You know that it is possibly Duff that messed with my house, right?"

Xera sighed and shook her head. "Yes, I know that he is not a good person and that Gideon has hinted at more, but he can't tell us the truth. All that cosmic role stuff. And his disappearing is definitely strange. The time stamp on it especially."

Xera stared up at him, tapping her fingers along his arm as she stood in thought. "Hear me out. I am not saying that all that isn't true or that he isn't some sort of demon or monster. However, aren't you the one always going on about proof and we have none that it was him or anything. He could just be some sort of flake that quit going to school. And I know Gideon told us he is more than we think and that, bless his heart, he can't tell us more, but still. He had so many chances to hurt me or kill me, and he never did. He has always looked out for me, even when he was being miserable, so."

Ryder chuckled and pulled her back toward him. "Always thinking and seeing the best in people, Xera. Gideon says there is a plan. There is more to it all. I wish he could tell us more, but unfortunately, part of our, whatever, fate or Destiny is to figure out everything ourselves. It's really unfair actually."

Xera shrugged. "Well, life isn't supposed to be easy for regular humans. What makes you think it would be any better for cosmic beings? It is probably worse actually."

Ryder cracked a smile at her brutal honesty and stared at her in the moonlight. He frowned when she shivered and decided time was up, they needed to go home before she got frozen. He tugged at her hand.

"Come on, Xera. Let's get you home. You have class in the morning, and it is cold. You are limping."

Ryder shivered in the dark as they walked. He paused for a moment, looking all around as he felt the hairs on the back of his neck rise and fall. Something or someone was watching them, but he couldn't pinpoint where. He shook his head and continued forward, holding fast to Xera's hand.

Perhaps Xera is right. I need to stop this searching. I am becoming paranoid and anxious. Seeing ghosts and shadows in the dark where there are none. It will all come back to me in time. I hope, anyway. We shall see.

Chapter 40

Xera & Duff

Xera slid into her cold living room. She started toward the fire, letting out a small groan as her leg stiffened. She stared down at the floor as she paused to rub at the knee, digging her fingers into it, massaging it all around.

"I really need to do something about this weather. Keep my fire banked or something. This is going to be painful until I get the fire started."

Xera grumbled at the fire as she bent to the task, piling the paper and wood all in to get it started. As the fire began to spark and smolder and the heat washed over her, she sighed happily.

I shouldn't have gone to see Ryder today, but I missed him and I adore seeing him. He was clearly happy to see me too. With the winter break upon us, not many people need his library skills, so he is adrift. I should have gone home for break, but to what? An empty house with broken promises and sad memories. No, I'll take the new good memories over those, despite that the memories with Mom are lovely.

Xera was thrown from her thoughts by a knock at her door. She frowned and pushed to her feet, tears springing to her eyes as pain lanced up her leg and down again. When she opened it, she came face to face with a delivery driver.

She stared at him. There was something familiar about him. The haughty look in his eyes and the tilt to his chin. She shrugged, probably nothing.

"Hello, can I help you?"

The man smiled and held out a small package. "Xeraphina McCall, I am Tyson, and I have your delivery from natural herbs and supplements."

Xeraphina smiled. "Oh. Wonderful. My tea came early. I wasn't expecting this for a few days."

The young man shrugged. "We had a few extra deliveries today that came early. I just need you to sign here, please, ma'am."

He held out a clipboard and offered her a smile. Xera signed her name with a flourish and took the small package.

She grasped her tea and, after shutting the door, went straight for the kitchen.

Ah, wonderful. I love my tea; it soothes my nerves. Now to find some of those pills of mine while the water is heating.

Xera took her first sip after sitting down and frowned. *This tea tastes different. I am not going to be happy if they changed their recipe. I will have to call them. Their number, I believe it is beside my computer.*

Xera frowned again and stared at the cup as her vision swam. She shook her head, dispelling the blurriness of her gaze. She stood up, trying to get to her living room and her phone, but the cup fell to the floor and shattered below her feet. She gasped lightly and fell to her knees. She crawled, finally reaching the door, but she could no longer move. She lifted her head once to gaze into the face of Duff and she cried out, but then her vision swam again and darkness pervaded her senses, and she remembered no more.

Duff stood staring down at Xera as she lay on the floor. He curled his lip at her and snarled deep within his throat.

"You have caused way too many problems, you damnable woman. Now you will pay for it."

He shook his head and smirked. *To think she*

had no idea who I was. Such weak eyes the mortals have with their need to see what they want to see. She couldn't see my face for what it was. It's a shame, really. This was almost too easy. What's the point of a hunt if there is no challenge? Well, let's clean this cup up and get the angel's little lover to the ritual site. The time is upon us. My Tamesis, she will have the immortality she so wants. And I will help her get it.

Duff picked up the pieces of china one by one, tossing them into the trash. He stared at the offending colors and shook his head. "Could you have at least picked out better-looking china? These are ugly."

Duff looked around one last time, making sure nothing looked out of place. Then, bending down, he picked up Xera and swung her over his broad shoulders. He grunted and growled out, "Much heavier than you look, angel."

Duff whistled as he walked, a smile on his face. It wasn't every day that you got to give your beloved what she wanted most in the world and today he could do just that. So far, it had gone without a hitch. Tamesis was waiting in the spot she had picked out for the ritual.

For a while there I wasn't sure if my Tamesis would ever get better again, not after Mother's torture. But now as things are starting to look up, she is almost better than she was. Happy and ready to begin this ritual, to become immortal.

Duff frowned as Xera began to stir, and he stopped long enough to smack her in the head. She cursed once and then passed out again. He smirked. "You know, Tamesis just needs you alive, not whole, so if I were you, I would stay asleep, although I wouldn't mind giving you a few more knocks to that dear little head of yours. You deserve them after all."

He had to stop a few more times. The last time he felt flesh give away beneath his fingers. He sighed and touched her throat. Her pulse was there, but it wasn't as fast. "Hopefully that knock holds. One more like that and I fear you are done for. I guess if I have to I can take you in kicking and screaming. Sweet justice if you ask me."

Duff slid into the broken-down mansion and tossed her to the stone slab, shackling her hands and feet to the table and smiled at his mate while she muttered under her breath and pattered from one end of the room to the other, keeping all her instruments ready to go.

"Hello, Tamesis, my love."

Tamesis looked at him and smiled, holding up the black dagger and licking the tip of the blade. "It's sharp enough. Time is of the essence. Was her fallen there or did you get her here without raising alarm?"

Duff shrugged and leaned against the stone walls, watching Xera to make sure she didn't move. A small stirring of pity touched his senses, but he pushed it aside. Now was not the time for such foolish human emotions.

"All went well, but that doesn't mean it will stay well. One of the two guardians will know she is missing soon enough, and then we will have a fight on our hands. I am hoping it won't be for some time. I left the house looking as if she was just out and about for a bit. That will keep them fooled for a bit, but not long."

Duff chewed on a thick slab of jerky he had pulled from a pocket and waited for Tamesis to speak, but she didn't. She just nodded along with what he was saying.

"Okay, all is well. The ritual will begin soon enough. Duff, go watch for the guardian. I'll call you if I need you, if she stirs."

Duff turned and ambled back down the stairs. Hopefully, they would not come looking for some time. But he didn't hold his breath on it; they were wily ones, the guardians. Always seemed to know everything, before sometimes even the dark ones did.

CHAPTER 41

XERA

Xera shifted, trying to get comfortable. She had been having a lovely dream about Ryder. *Ryder.* Her eyes burst open, she breathed heavily as she stared up at a strange ceiling. She bit her lip to keep from moaning at the pain that radiated from her head to her legs and back up again. She pushed back, trying to relieve the pressure in her back, and she growled at the sharp pain that shot up her spine.

She turned her head a small amount, squinting her eyes against the dimly lit room. She nibbled at her lip and tried to move her hand to brush a strand of hair from her eyes, but she was momentarily struck dumb as she met resistance. Something heavy and cumbersome took up the space on her wrist. She cut her eyes down and felt panic start to well in her breast as she stared at the heavy manacles that chained her to the stone table. They held her arms in place, but if she moved there was wiggle room for her wrist.

If only I could figure out a way to slide my hands free. I would need something slippy, like dish soap. All out of that, though.

Xera took deep, steadying breaths while tears leaked from beneath her eyes. She had to try all manners of calming her nerves. While deep inside she wanted to panic. She shook her head and slowly looked around the room, shivering as a heavy wind blew through and curled around her. She cursed under her breath at the manacles that covered her wrists. She had wanted to curl her arms around herself, stop some of the chill from getting into her bones.

She stared at the high ceilings and the white, bare floor of what she could see. The white had char marks up and down its sides and large open windows with the glass broken out. She swallowed quickly. They looked like fearsome eyes looking out into the beyond. She shivered again and jumped at the first sound of laughter near her right side.

Xera tilted her head, searching for the owner of the malicious and cruel laugh with the high, girlish quality. The laughter squeezed her heart like cold fingers while it skittered up her spine like ice. The owner moved in the shadows, and Xera squinted her eyes harder, trying to see the person's face. When the young woman stepped into view, Xera screamed as loud as she could. The face that stared at her was her own, but it was so vastly different. Broken down and marred with marks from something she wasn't sure. Long scars traced their way up and down the other woman's body, along her arms, and deep into her chest. Xera could see the risen pink on the top of the woman's v-neck shirt.

"Shut up."

Xera whimpered as her twin slapped her across the face. "You know, I admired you once upon a time, though maybe we could be sisters, but then I realized, no. You are far too cowardly and weak, Xeraphina McCall. But, well met regardless. I am your twin sister. Tamesis Jade. Strange, isn't it, to see your face on another."

Xera shuddered as the woman grew nearer and stared at her, moving her eyes restlessly over Xera's face. "But your face, so unmarked, and that body too. And, well, you will give that to me."

Xera struggled against her bonds, a deep keening sound in her throat as she fought to get away, both from the woman and her softly spoken words. Talking to her as if they were best friends.

Tamesis moved closer, pulling a chair to sit beside Xera. "I have such big plans, sister, such big plans."

Xera shifted, pushing herself as far away from the other as she could. Tamesis rubbed her hands together and smiled, her eyes lighting up with a maniacal light and glimmering darkly at Xera.

Xera looked around, trying to figure out what to do, trying to remember all the training from all the different classes on self-defense. She opened her mouth and choked out a few questions, pushing past the lump that sat in her throat, hard and cruel.

"How didn't I know about you? Where are you from, uh, Tamesis?"

As Xera waited for the other to speak, she continued to look around, trying to find any way to break free.

"No need to worry about such things, dear sister." Tamesis played with a small dagger back and forth in her hands, moving it around and lifting it to study it in the dim light. Tamesis smiled insanely and continued. "I see you watching all around you, little mousey, mousey, but this cat has you cold locked. You are going nowhere. You will give me your blood and with it, your immortality. It is a shame I must wait a little while longer, but, well, these rituals, after all, they have to be followed to the letter."

Xera swallowed thickly again and stared after Tamesis as the woman stood up and moved around the room, scratching the letter T into all the surfaces.

"Why would you want to kill me? Surely –"

Tamesis screeched in rage and flew across the room, giving Xera a glancing blow to her head, making her ears ring. "Shut your trap, whore. I have had enough of this chit chat. You will die, and I will be the one to do it. I already told you, your immortality is what I am after."

Xera tugged half-heartedly at her shackles, knowing they would not give way. Tamesis stared at her and sneered. "Such a fool you are, Xera. So much given to you and you don't even appreciate it, none of you. Not yourself or your precious fallen librarian or even your old guardian. All of you fools. So much to take, the souls of the world have so much to give and you all prance around with self-righteous views of right and wrong, when there is neither, only those powerful and those too weak to seek the power. You are the latter, in case you are wondering, wench."

Tamesis bent forward and traced circled along her sister's skin but making sure not to cut it. Xera growled at the cold steel against her flesh. "You know, Xera, that man of yours. Maybe I should see if Lilith will let me have him for fun. Surely Duff would allow it too. You know that I could make him moan and whine with need. I can make him want me so badly that he cannot think straight for the need. I could make him hate the very air you breathed. Should I do that, Xera?"

Tamesis kissed her cheek and nipped at her ear as she moved past. "Well, should I?"

Xera screamed again in fury and fought against her shackles. "When I get a hold of you…"

Tamesis chuckled darkly. "Ah, that is the fight I like to see. Funny thing, love, it changes things, doesn't it?"

Xera growled again and fought against her shackles harder. "Oh Xera, you won't break them. It's really a shame that your angel isn't here to watch the light leave your eyes."

Xera shuddered again, and Tamesis grinned at her, rubbing her head and patting her shoulder. "You have twenty minutes left on this earth. Anything to say, twinny dear?"

Xera twisted her head and sneered. "I will kill you, Tamesis."

Tamesis laughed. "You won't have a chance."

A loud scream of fury was heard throughout the night, and Xera smiled to herself. "Looks like my angel is on his way, Tamesis."

Tamesis slapped her in the face, making her head bounce against the stone slab. Xera groaned and stars danced behind her eyes. She tried to quiet the ringing in her ears, but it intensified, so she lay still, controlling her breathing.

She took one deep breath and screamed for all she was worth for Ryder. Then she lay back and closed her eyes, fighting the overwhelming urge to throw up.

CHAPTER 42

RYDER

Ryder scrubbed at the blood on his hands as he rushed toward the empty, burned out husk of a mansion at the end of town. He had known it was evil but had been unsure how. Tonight, he had awoken from a much-needed nap and realized most of what he was and the secrets that were hidden. It was as if the awakening wakened something deep within. It was the thousandth day of the thousandth year and his and Xera's last chance at redemption and forgiveness. He was still unsure how he had to win both, but he knew that he would do it, because this was the last time, the last free ride.

His mind wandered to Gideon and the older man lying in his own blood. The wounds that were inflicted upon him made Ryder's stomach turn. He hadn't seen those types in some time, and to do so on neutral ground... When he found out who had done it, he would make them pay for it, only as a Guardian could make a wrongdoer feel it. Gideon had managed to choke out to him of the mansion and Xera; they had Xera. Then the old man had waved him on, telling him to hurry, he could heal himself with help from others who were coming.

I hope the old man will be okay. I will never forgive myself if I left him to his death. But right now, Xera needs me, before Duff and whatever a soulless is harms her. That is what Gideon murmured.

Ryder increased his speed and, at the first scream, he cried out and ran even faster, his chest heaving in exertion and the tell-tale burn in his lungs. He was a man in shape, but even he got tired.

Ryder skidded to a stop and stared at the mansion. The ash stirred as he walked forward, anxious to be as quiet as he could. He touched a hand to the back of his clothes, making sure that the daggers were still there. A gift from Gideon, before he told him to go. Their obsidian color was a startling contrast to the bright white gems that lay in the center. But they felt comfortable in his hand and on his person. Ryder pushed through the creaking door, wincing as it made a small whisper of a sound. He searched the nooks and crannies, looking for shadows that could be there to pounce. He heard the stirring of voices above him and the loud scream of Xera. He howled out her name, no longer caring if anyone heard. The sound of a hand hitting flesh had Ryder seeing red, and he pushed himself further up the staircase, anxious to get to her. Her scream came again for him and, following it, Duff came running from the room at the top of the rickety stairs. Ryder stared at him and lowered his gaze, furious.

Duff smirked and held out his hand. "Precious fallen. How wonderful it is to see you."

Ryder stared at him, repulsed, for his glamor no longer hid his face from view. Ryder snarled at the face of black with the glowing green eyes and red claws.

"Oh, I remember you now, son of Lilith, demon of chaos and ruin. I remember you well. I believe I have taken your life as many times as you have taken mine."

Ryder saw a flicker of fear burn in the creature's eyes, but he hid it quickly. "Not tonight, fallen. Tonight, I will win, and it is the last time you will ever walk this earth or the heavens. You and your precious little whore will be no more, but me and mine, we will be strong again."

Ryder smiled coldly, pulling his daggers from his sheaths. "I will have my revenge, Duff. You have Xera; I'll take your head."

Duff simpered. "Should an angel speak of such things as revenge? Isn't that why you became what you are, almost one of us, but not quite yet."

Ryder grimaced but forced a laugh. "I fell from grace long ago."

Ryder felt the power building deep in his core, the want, no, the need to smite the creature that stared at him so boldly.

Ryder roared and ran up the steps, his daggers at the ready. Ryder surged forward and backed up as the creature swung his claws at his face. He swung up with his right hand, holding the dagger in a swipe, and batted with his left. Metal met metal and the grating noise put his teeth on edge.

Ryder moved his eyes from corner to corner, searching for a way to get past Duff. Duff swung with his claws, and Ryder pushed up and away, cutting under the demon's arm. He parried and backed up, moving away to secure his position. Crouching, he moved around the other, only to be blocked. Ryder growled and shifted, ready to attack again. Ryder slid forward again, countering. He thrust at the other's body and grappled with his other hand.

He could hear someone softly muttering and he swung again, anxious to get to Xera. Even if he couldn't kill Duff, all he needed was to get past him.

Xera struggled against her bonds again and again, trying to force herself away from the table. She listened as her evil twin murmured and chanted under her breath. Repeating over and over again the same things.

"Midnight, Midnight. Must wait until Midnight. The ritual must be right, just a little longer, just some time, that is all we need."

Xera stared as the other woman rang her hands and then would rub them across her sides only to do it all over again.

Xera's blood ran cold as Tamesis continued to growl and moan under her breath about fallen angels and the last angels to walk among them. Xera shifted and sighed when sharp pains ran up and down her arms and legs. She had been used as a cutting board. Xera let out a sharp intake of breath as pain lanced up her arm from her wrist. Xera stared at the manacles and tried to think of a way to slide her hand free. She caught sight of a nail, jutting from the table top. She stared at her wrist in horror.

I suppose though being maimed is better than being dead.

She whimpered as she began to slide her wrist

against the sharp metal. The first bite of metal, made her wince and she closed her eyes tight, stopping the scream from bursting forth. Xera moved her wrist up and down, wincing at the pain that lanced up each time as she moved it across a nail fastened to the shackles. She let out a small, triumphant squeal when her slippery red hand slid free. She stopped, frozen in place and looked at Tamesis, making sure she did not see her.

Xera sighed in relief as the woman continued to rant and rave while watching the battle below ensue. Xera could not see it, but each grunt and howl of pain made her wince and sigh, hoping that Ryder was okay. The clang of weapons below rang throughout the building.

Xera stared in disgust at the other manacle that traced her delicate wrist. Doing the same thing, she yelped when the skin tore, but she pulled it free as well. Contorting painfully, she bent to undo the shackles on her legs; the key had been recklessly placed near her. She bit her lip to keep from crying out as her body sang out in protest, the numerous wounds that bathed her body made rivulets of blood fall to the ground and all around. Finally freed, she stood up on shaky legs and stared at Tamesis and the doorway.

What now, Xera? Do I try and help Ryder or do I dispose of this woman? I don't think I could kill someone, even though she would definitely deserve it.

Xera walked on tiptoe toward Tamesis, wincing at each step as pain radiated up her legs. And the blood that slid down her arms. She would need to get them bound soon. She looked around her searching for something. She saw a nearby cloth, probably used to clean a wound. Grasping it she wound it around her mangled right wrist. She bit her lip looking for another. She saw nothing and sighed. Eyes darted from table to table, finally falling onto a small dagger placed near her. Probably the same implement that had left the marks in her legs and arms. Grasping it, she held it in front of her. Indecision weighing her down.

She froze when Ryder bellowed in pain and anger and something deep within Xera snapped. Snarling, she launched herself at Tamesis. Throwing her arms around her neck, she pulled her backward, grappling with her, trying to gain a foothold to get to Ryder, to get past her.

Ryder fought claw against dagger, every clang, every yelp making his teeth set further on edge. He could smell the blood in the air, and he knew it was Xera's and it drove him mad with fear. What would he find when he finally made it to the top of the stairs and into the room?

Ryder looked up and froze, almost costing him

his arm when he stared at the woman that stood in the doorway watching them. It looked exactly like Xera, but her face was so scarred and her body... He stared and then grabbed the stairs to keep from falling down them. It was as if in slow motion he watched as two paler arms encircled the woman in the door frame and she was pulled back with a howl of fury.

Ryder smiled hard and breathed out his beloved's name. "Xera."

Duff too heard the cry and turned to look at the doorway, a movement that would cost him. Ryder bent forward and slammed into demon, knocking him backward. He pushed past the demon, knocking him to the ground with a hard elbow between the eyes. He pushed past and into the doorway, his heart hammering deep within his chest. He searched the gloomy darkness for any sign of Xera.

Ryder stared in abject horror as Xera and her twin fought in the corner, Xera using a small dagger while Tamesis swung a cruel looking black dagger. Ryder rushed forward to help but roared in pain when a large claw clapped upon his shoulder and dug in. Duff pulled him backward and pushed him against the wall, digging his claws into his shoulders and twisting. Ryder screamed in pain but fought to gain a foothold and jerked the claws from his arms with a howl.

Ryder stared at Xera, watching as his beautiful guardian angel stood toe to toe, with blood dripping from numerous wounds. She fought on hard. Ryder gained a new wind and shoved at Duff, slamming the other man in the head multiple times as hard as he could, the blows jolting his arm and making him wince.

Doesn't matter. I must get to Xera. I need to get to her. She needs me. I need to save her.

Ryder watched in horror as Tamesis swung her dagger and gave Xera a glancing blow to her shoulder. Ryder roared, but he was cut short from moving by the large, meaty claw of Duff. He turned back to fight with him, his body aching and his heart heavy. He needed to get to Xera.

Xera howled and grasped her shoulder, digging her fingers into the wound, blood flowing through her pale fingers to splash heavy and red against the ground. She pushed against the wall, Tamesis pushing at her, forcing her into the wall. Xera searched behind her for a weapon or a window ledge, anything to get away from Tamesis.

Xera saw it coming before it came, the candle light dancing along Tamesis's black blade, arching and snapping, and Xera tripped into the open window. The searing pain that came when the knife plunged made her scream. Her throat felt as if the tissue and skin were giving away beneath its power. Golden sparks gleamed along the blade from Xera's wound, lighting up the area around her. Xera cried out as the golden sparks settled onto Tamesis and she watched in horror as her twin sister grappled at her throat and chest. Finally, she fell to the ground gasping for air. The magic that she had touched too much for her to bear. Xera sighed, tears streaming from her eyes.

Xera felt empty air behind her, and she stared at Ryder, a small smile on her face. They had won; he had finally let her make her own choice to die. He allowed her to sacrifice herself finally to save him. Smiling at him, she let go of the ledge and began a free fall to the ground; she would be dead long before she made it, though.

Light poured from her chest to light up the darkness around her as she fell. She heard the cry of Ryder as he rushed to the window, but she closed her eyes. She had saved him; he was a fallen no more.

Chapter 43

Ryder

Ryder saw the glancing blow to Xera and with a roar, he ran toward the window. Ash and sparks lit up the room around him. He rushed forward, reaching to the window but all he met was open air. He howled in fury and fear and grief, and he saw light dancing along the night air as Xera fell. He howled again and dropped his daggers.

Ryder grabbed the ledge, holding tight, his fingers grew white and he stared up at the heavens and roared at them. He hadn't prayed in years, but as Xera fell, he prayed to them all. The council, the gods, whoever could hear him. He prayed as hard as he could, the words forming faster than he could even manage to repeat.

Ryder turned to look at Duff once, and the

creatures broken face made Ryder sigh. There was no hate for the thing anymore. To lose someone you loved, that was punishment enough. Ryder knew that well. He turned and jumped out the window himself. He prayed again to his mother, his father, whoever could hear him and possibly save his Xera.

Ryder fell, holding his arms straight down. He growled under his breath as his back began to sting and smart, smoke and light billowing on all sides, and with a scream of pain, his shirt began to rip. The skin of his back and its scars tore open and tears sprang to his eyes as finally, they separated and, with a bright, golden light and a snap, his wings unfurled. The feathery down wings he had earned back. The wings from his dreams black with one white band around the middle, showing that he was more than just an angel, that he was a guardian, son of Kavi Greer. Both light and dark warred within him. He was neither fallen nor angel nor mortal, but all three. He was the last Guardian to walk the earth.

Ryder folded his wings to his back and went straight down, not toward hell, but rather toward the small slice of heaven that he could physically hold, the one piece that loved him with no conditions. A lump formed in his throat and his eyes burned with the wind and the unshed tears, but he needed to get to Xera. It was only a matter of time before she succumbed to the wounds that made up her body, and he wanted to tell her he loved her one more time and hear it back.

Ryder grasped her and gently pulled her into his arms, and he held her there aloft. She nuzzled his arm and smiled weakly. "Oh, Ryder. So wonderful to see your beautiful wings. I love you."

Ryder cried out as she whimpered, and he held her closer. Though he knew she would become an angel and still be there, it hurt to watch her die. "I love you too."

Ryder landed to the ground gently, holding Xera in his arms. He knew who he was again, knew he was Ryder Greer, the wise warrior, the guardian angel, and in his arms, he held his own guardian angel. She had, however, guarded much more than just his soul. She had guarded his heart for a thousand years.

Ryder stood with his wings folded gently over them. Ryder winced and growled as he looked to his arm and he watched in fascination as a dove adorned in gold began to form on his arm. A dove for his soul, the powerful soul he had finally unleashed and learned to forgive.

Ryder jumped as above him a loud howl rent the air. Duff finally allowing his grief to penetrate the world. Ryder shuddered as his howl again filled up the night, and he sighed. He brushed at his eyes.

"I hated him once, but to lose your love… I can't hate him anymore."

Another shriek filled the air and Ryder pulled Xera to his chest, looking all around. He knew that screech, knew who it was before the smell of sulfur and decaying leaves filled the air.

Lilith stood in front of him and reached toward him when suddenly, Gideon was there in a blaze of white light, and he covered them both with his golden wings.

"No, lover of Cain. You own no one here. They do not belong to you. We have won."

Lilith scowled and crossed her arms, but Gideon continued.

"See that golden aura around Xera? It means she is dying, but she is also one of us. You have lost, damned one."

Ryder stared in confusion and mild amusement as the queen of darkness threw a child-like tantrum, full with stomping her feet and screaming at the top of her lungs.

"All my planning! It was so perfect."

She stared at Ryder and snarled. "You may have one Greer, spawn, but I will gain more souls. There are endless mortals out there, and I will sway them to the dark side. I will stop at nothing to destroy you and all you stand for. You will pay for all your sins against me. The humiliation of lying beneath a man. The deaths of thousands of my children. I will ruin you all"

She turned and with another snarl, her sharp fangs showing up, she disappeared into shadows, the smell of decay and sulfur pervading the area.

Ryder shifted, and Xera looked up at Gideon, but she could not even lift her head. Instead, she smiled kindly.

"Gideon." The small tone of her voice made Ryder's heart clench. He brushed at his eyes again, trying to dispel the tears that threatened to soak them both.

Gideon moved forward and put a hand on Ryder's shoulder, squeezing kindly.

"Oh Xera, my sweet child. I am very sorry that you must die again, but I am so glad that this time, your death is not in vain. This time we have won."

Gideon touched her head gently. "You are truly one of the blessed, my dear, and I award you one of our greatest honors. A gift only given to a few of our greatest guardian angels. You will receive the golden wings of sacrifice, and there is no one more deserving than you, my dear girl."

Gideon stepped away from her, and Ryder was momentarily blinded as a golden light lit up the space around them. Xera was lifted from his arms. He cried out, but a sigh of relief left his chest when her two hands found his arms and squeezed.

He closed his eyes, rubbing at them. When he opened them, Xera stood in front him whole and adorning her back were wide wings of golden feathers. She was beautiful.

Gideon smiled and placed his hand on Ryder's arm. "Ah, it is so good to see the two of you so whole. Xera, my dear, I have one more gift for you. Well, not a gift, but rather giving back something that is yours. And Ryder, my boy, you have done well, you with your path of life inked into your broken skin, the only guardian to wear his life so proudly."

Gideon touched her head, and Ryder rushed forward to hold her upright as she bent forward, thousands of years of lifetimes passing before her eyes. Ryder shuddered. He would be next and, all too soon, he was. He gasped as they danced along his eyelids, and when he was done, he stood hands on his knees, panting.

Ryder stood staring at his mate and his mentor, a smile on his face, but slowly, he began to frown. He cleared his throat and looked to Gideon. "Gideon, I have not quite figured out something. Can I ask you a question?"

Gideon chuckled. "Always with the questions, my boy, but proceed."

Ryder ran his hand across his face, rubbing the scar that took up most of it. "How did Tamesis exist? I mean, wouldn't Xera and I have remembered a twin, even now with all of our memories back? I remember nothing of her."

Gideon looked to Ryder, meeting his gaze, and he rubbed his chin. "That is a hard question to answer. Why is it you always choose the hard ones to ask? Ever since you were a boy."

"She has always been there, but not in the capacity that you think. You have to remember that when you two were born thousands of years ago, it was very rare for twins to survive past birth. There was always one stronger twin that lived. That twin was Xera."

Ryder shifted, and Xera leaned into him as they listened. "She was always destined to die, but at some point, Lilith, feeling that we played unfairly, decided to unbalance things in her own way. She allowed the child to survive, but at a terrible cost: she had no soul. She went through life unable to feel much of anything but anger and revenge and discontent bred in her heart."

Ryder stared at Gideon, but before he could say anything to him, a man with jet black angel wings materialized in front of him. The black wings that adorned his back, lackluster and dull, but still intact. The other man's face was so scarred it was hard to discern exactly what he was looking at, but Ryder could see glimpses of himself in his father's face.

His father moved forward and grasped his arm, pulling him and Xera both into a hug.

"Hello, you two. Though you will never hear it from the council. I am very proud of you and they are too, even if they don't admit it. You two have done so well. It amazes me and kills me all at once. To think of the abuse you had to endure."

Ryder stared at his father as the old man's lip trembled, and he shifted. "Anyway, I have come to bring the two of you home. It is time to ascend to heaven and there you shall gain your just reward and your new charges."

Ryder looked one last time at the ground around him, the library, and he sighed, Grasping Xera's hand, he followed her into the light and what awaited them there.

About the Author

Layne Calry is a working mom of three boys under the age of six. She has been writing since she was fourteen and finished her first novel at twenty-four. Layne loves to write longhand outside under the trees while her children play. Layne holds an Associate's Degree in Business Management and Health Administration, and she plans to continue with more school later on. Layne is from rural Pennsylvania where she still can be found to this day, usually in bare feet and outside. Layne has two publication, both short stories titled "Saul's Betrayal" and "Darkness Closes In." They can be found in the anthologies Betrayals of Another Kind and Forbidden Rites, both compiled by J.E. Feldman.